THE
BLACK HAWKS

by
VITO QUATTROCCHI

This is a work of fiction. Any names, characters, places, and incidents are either
the product of the author's imagination or are used fictitiously. Any
resemblance to events or persons, living or dead, is entirely coincidental.

Published in 2006 by

Suburban Enterprises

VtQuattrocchi@yahoo.com

14800 4400 300 500 6200 8312

Foreword

In the 1960s and 70's Hudson County New Jersey youth gangs' ethnicity ranged from Italian, Irish, Puerto Rican to Polish. Some of the individual members of the gangs were from different races such as Dominican, Cuban, German and Albanian. The Italian gangs dominated Hudson County at that time. These were the Golden Guineas, The Gladiators, Black Hawks, Jackson Street Gents, Iron Dukes, Monroe Street Buddies and the Red Circle Gang, The Marion boys from Jersey City. Many of these youth gangs served as feeder gangs into the Italian Mafia. Those feeder gangs that led into the Italian Mafia were called 'Hard Gangs.' Of course not anyone could just work with the Mafia, only boys who were smart enough or tough enough were asked to be involved. As they grew up, the boys were observed by the mobsters as they rubbed shoulders in pool rooms and bars scattered across the city. If anyone showed promise, the mobsters took mental notes and eventually asked the person in question to help him in activities like running numbers and making collections. This books focus in on one street gang in particular from Hoboken New Jersey, "The Black Hawks," a Hard gang or feeder gang into a particular Mafia family "The Messian Family". *For futher reading on the Messina family read "Sins of The Fathers" by Vito Quattrocchi, LuLu Publishing.*

Northern New Jersey
City of Hoboken 1966

Hoboken, New Jersey 1966, an urban American slum in the looming shadow of Manhattan. A town of blue collar immigrants where organized crime, mainly the Italian Mafia, controlled and manipulated everything. Street crime was not only lucrative but a way of life in these immigrant communities. The majority of street crime and gang activity in Hudson County, New Jersey, shifted to the teenage world of minors, some as young as 12 years old. They were not only committing vastly more gang-related crimes, but deadlier. As younger and younger members clambered to join street gangs, more teens were getting arrested and even killed. The police were overwhelmed, dealing with the growing number of juvenile crime rings.

These teenage street gangs headquartered in every neighborhood; each club on their own turf. The Black Hawks,(Italian) the Lords,(Italian) - the Red Circle Gang (Italian) - the Iron Dukes (Italian) - the Alkies (Puerto Rican) - the Crazy Eights (Puerto Rican) – Latin Kings(Hispanic) – Pagans(Black and Hispanic). As members of other crews were constantly beefing up and shifting alliances as each gang jockeyed for position. The gangs worked the streets, running numbers, selling spread sheets, dealing drugs and carrying guns.

The Black Hawks, the primary Italian street gang in Hoboken, New Jersey, did their hanging out in front of a storefront club room on Friday and Saturday nights talking street gossip, rackets, crap games, about guys who were made, about guys who got wacked and the money that could be made from one sweet move. Their voices purposely inflecting the hard Italian American street dialect of Northern New Jersey. [1]

The age range was sixteen to twenty, spoiling for a fight; swift and merciless, an uppercut to the groin, a chop behind the ear, a few well placed kicks and it was over, a savagery not tempered by youth; bodies hard, eyes narrow and cruel. Alert and tense, smoking endlessly, fanatical about their dress; pastel Italian knit shirts with matching pants, see through silk socks and straw shoes. The Nicky Newark look, really sharp.

"Hey Nicky, wadda ya know?"

"Nothin, I didn't see nothin! I know nothin and I'm not saying nothin! *Omerta!*[2]" This wisdom kept street kids alive and kept them street kids.

---

1   A mixture of Italian and English words jumbled together to form a sub-linguistic dialect exclusive to the Italian American communities of New York and North Jersey.
2   *Omerta:* The Sicilian code of scilence.

Chapter 1

Hoboken New Jersey
1966

Vito Fierro lit a non filter Lucky Strike cigarette, inhaled deeply, letting the smoke out through his nose. He took a wad of money out of his pocket and undid the rubber band that held the bills, counting out his cash. He was happy with the fact that he had acquired this money without having to work for it. Only suckers worked a nine to five job, getting bossed around by some asshole who thought you were his slave for a friggin dollar sixty an hour.

This week he was passing counterfeit bills. He procured this money from Jo-Jo Manetti, a local hood that dealt in fraudulent currency. A hundred dollars to Jo-Jo gave Vito three hundred in counterfeit. Then, he would buy a five dollar item, paying with a fake twenty dollar bill and receive fifteen dollars back in real cash as change. It was a good deal for Vito and he was happy as he looked at his newly purchased 14 karat gold I.D. bracelet. It was a thick, Cuban link chain with a heavy plate across the top and small diamonds spelling out "Vito" across the plate. He purchased it on Canal Street in Manhattan just across the river, a bus ride away from downtown Hoboken. The I.D bracelet was a real beauty.

"Got a new I.D.?" One of the Black Hawks[3] asked him.

---

3   BlackHawks, a North Jersey, Hoboken Street gang.

"Yeah," Vito nodded. "Got it on Canal Street at one of those Chink jewelry stores, only paid half a yard[4] for it."

The Hawk held Vito's wrist and examined the bracelet. "Not bad kid," he finally said. "Ya know you can mess somebody up really good with this if ya want to. It's thick enough, just put the plate over your knuckles and slug a guy in the mouth. This piece will smash the bastard's teeth. Good luck with it."

"Thanks," said Vito, reverently.

The Hawk nodded at Vito and refused the cigarette Vito offered him. "Try one of these." He extended his gold cigarette case to Vito. "Take one, it's a marijuana joint. If ya gonna smoke, it might as well do something for ya."

Vito balked, shaking his head. "Nah, I don't think so." The Hawk's look became hard and accusing.

"What's the matter?" He asked slowly. "Afraid? We ain't got room for mutts in the Black Hawks!"

Vito nodded and lit the joint. The Hawk slapped him on the back, encouragingly. "Did you get your piece yet kid?"

"Yeah," Vito nodded, "I got it on Mulberry Street, one of the Goomba kids sold it to me. It's a beauty." Vito took out his newly purchased 22. caliber revolver and showed it proudly to the Hawk.

"Good, kid, good. You'll be a Hawk soon enough. Just enjoy that weed and come down to the club room. Make sure you talk to Aldo; you're the kind of guy we want in the Black Hawks." He slapped Vito's shoulder, "smoke that bone," he laughed, walking away.

Okay, so what, Vito thought, this is no big deal. Everybody smokes this shit. If you wanted to be in with the guys, you couldn't be afraid of anything. He pushed his way into the crowd walking along Washington Avenue. Any night of the week, but especially on

---

4   Half a yard, slang for $500 dollars.

7

Friday and Saturday nights, the avenue was a vibrant street with a mass of shoppers and strollers and hang out guys who walked with purpose. Both sides of Washington Avenue were lined with stores and restaurants and club rooms. Radios from second story windows blared Spanish music. The Puerto Ricans always blasted their music as if everyone wanted to listen to their shit. However, it did lend a kind of excitement to the environment.

"Fucking Spics," he thought. They were the enemy and the niggers too; both of them fucked up the entire projects. Downtown was okay before they came into the neighborhood. The State bussed them in from Newark and gave them low income housing in the Marshall Drive Projects. Now, they were making it a shit hole. But the Italian gangs had the town sewn up and that's all that mattered.

Vito turned down Fourth Street towards Adams Street. He walked with his hands in his pockets holding his newly purchased 22. caliber pistol, his eyes alert for rival gangs. He stayed alert until he saw the spiral of Saint Ann's Roman Catholic Church, the epicenter of his neighborhood. For in 1966, downtown Hoboken, was a wasted, hopeless, neighborhood with home relief and welfare as its principal occupations. The Vietnam War was in full swing and the only escape from the low income tenements was military enlistment. Rival gangs fought for dominance of the streets. Mostly Hispanic and Italian gangs vied, both jockeying for position. In ever increasing numbers, people left the slums of Hoboken for better lives in the surrounding suburbs, as they could afford to move.

Vito's father had worked in the shipyards passing out tools to the mechanics making non union wage. Eventually, he got busted for taking bets and booking numbers in order to supplement his meager income. He was sentenced to three years on gambling charges. Hopefully, he would be out in nine months on good behavior. Meanwhile, his mother worked double shifts as a sewing-machine operator in a factory that made woman's clothes. Even though she worked overtime, money was tight. The arguments at home became worse and worse, until their Monroe Street flat always seemed to be filled with the loud voice and shrill screams of his mother complaining that there wasn't enough money and what was Vito doing to help out around the place? What was he doing buying gold bracelets and hanging around on street corners when they needed the basic necessities of life? Sometimes, the tension was so great he thought that he would lose his mind.

However, as he walked down the street with money in his pocket, that unpleasantness was all forgotten. In the back of his mind, thoughts were buried that he did not want to think about but could not really forget. One thought was when he remembered the cheap twenty five dollar Confirmation suit that his father had bought for him for which he had to take a million dollars' worth of crap from the guys at school who had better suits than him. Another was when he thought about the food stamps, the cheap clothes and sneakers bought at "John's Bargain Store" on First Street. There was continual complaining that there wasn't enough money for the things they needed. That's when Vito would seek refuge on the corner of his block and stand with the dopes and the beta males, watching the alpha males in the gangs. He would get nervous and stutter when one of the gang members would nod at him or even ask him for a cigarette.

Now, however, he was sixteen. Maybe the guys would permit him to hang around more often and let him into the crew. Soon, he hoped he would be considered one of the gang; solid and accepted with the right guys. The main Italian gang in Hoboken was the "Black Hawks" or the "Hawks" as they were generally called. Each member of the Hawks had to own a pistol, that was a vital requirement. And now, Vito had his piece tucked in his right hand

9

pants pocket. He had purchased it in Little Italy on Mulberry Street in Manhattan just up from Canal street where he bought his new I.D. bracelet. The 22. caliber pistol was a cheap nickle plated revolver, (*a Saturday Night Special*) but damn it if it still wasn't a pistol.

He walked with confidence down Monroe Street where the Hawks storefront clubroom was. The Black Hawks were a hard gang[5] and the biggest gang in downtown Hoboken. There were other gangs or "hard gangs" that were extensions of real Mafia crews. The Hawks were one of them. Aldo Pinto was the crew chief of the Black Hawks, since Tony Messina (founder of the crew) left the Black Hawks and went into the Army. Big Aldo Pinto took over as the Hawks titular president. Tony Messina's Uncle Franco ruled Hudson County, New Jersey's rackets, from gambling to prostitution to waste management and a hell of a lot more. Nothing came through Hoboken without Don Franco Messina's permission. So, the Black Hawks were under Don Franco's protection. That made the Hawks the most influential street gang in Hudson County, New Jersey. Vito wanted in more than he wanted to breath; for to be a Black Hawk meant money, respect, girls and just about everything a guy could want. Maybe there would be even enough money to move out of the tenements and get an apartment for his family uptown where it was nice and clean.

There was a gated section of Hoboken called "Castle Point" where the well-to-do lived. Its streets were gated off from the rest of Hoboken and its immigrant community. Castle Point had beautiful gray limestone and marble mansions with tall french windows in which hung heavy draperies that barred the sun and the prying gazes of the people who passed by. There were unlittered parks with benches that were invitingly empty and private. The apartment houses that overlooked the Hudson River had a view of the New

---

5   A Hard Gang – A street gang that is hooked up and has ties with a real Mafia family.

York City skyline. The tall apartments with their rooftop gardens and penthouses; things so distant and remote from Vito's imagination that his reaction was one of bitter irritation. As he looked at the quiet assurance of the handsome people standing under the canopies, strolling with dignity along the street, he saw only an affront, an affront to the misery, poverty and squalor which resided in the downtown area of Hoboken. It was all just so unfair. Why was it unfair? He did not know, but it was. Just because his mother and father were poor immigrants from Sicily was no reason why they had to live in a stinking, rotten tenement of blackened brick in a slum neighborhood. However, someday he would move away, yeah, someday he would maybe buy a fine flat on Castle Point and make his mother and father and little brother proud. Someday he would get the hell out of the frigging tenements.

Chapter 2

The next morning, Vito's little brother Dominic, lying on the other bed, sat up, stretched and yelled to Vito to get up and get ready for school. Dominic's bed was next to the window. He looked out over the fire escape on to the next tenement. Looking out of the adjacent window through the grates of the green rusted fire escape was Joey Pazzo staring at him from across the alley. As he caught Dominic's eye, he gave him the finger, mouthing the words, *"Tu madre e una putana!* (Your mother's a whore!)

"Vito", he called to his brother, "wake up! That idiot, Joey Pazzo, just gave me the finger and said, *Your mother is a whore.* I hate that idiot and all your stupid friends. Are you gonna let him say that about our mother?"

Vito rolled over, "What did he say?"

"He said in Italian, *Tu madre e una putana.* You should kick his stupid, crazy ass for that and if you don't you're a pussy.

"You better shut your mouth or I'll kick your ass, you little punk!" Vito swung his legs off the bed, moving towards his little brother.

Dominic held up his pillow to block the slap coming in his direction. "You better not hit me, or I'll tell mama. Why don't you hit that idiot, Joey? He's a piece of shit to say that about our mother and you want to hit me?"

"Shit," Vito said, "I wish we didn't have to live here. Why can't Momma and Poppa find a better place to live? Even when they were both working they couldn't afford higher rent. Shit, I hate this place!

Why did the cops have to bust Poppa?! It was just numbers! Fucking cops, I hate them!"

"Me too," said Dominic. "And most of all, I hate that crazy Joey! I wish I wasn't just ten years old! I'd kick his stupid ass myself!"

Vito got up off the bed. "Where the hell are my cigarettes?" he said, before answering him. "You're a shrimp and Joey wouldn't think twice about smashing your face, little guy or not. That bastard is a certifiable lunatic. Just leave him alone."

"Are you gonna make me breakfast?" Dominic asked Vito.

"Sure kid, what do you want? I can make you scrambled eggs with toast and butter."

"I wish Momma was home like she used to be and make me breakfast. Her cooking is the best. She always fries the eggs in olive oil and garlic. Boy, are they good."

"Shut up about Momma being home. When she wasn't out working, we didn't have enough to eat. Now, at least, our fridge is full. Just let me wash up first, then I'll make something for you."

Quickly, he washed his hands and arms and soaped his armpits. The room in which they slept was close and hot. He wanted to be clean and fresh for school. He rubbed 'Groom and Clean Pomade' in his dark hair, combing it back Italian style and checking his look in the mirror.

The first and most lasting impression of Vito's appearance was that of hardness, a look that he practiced and perfected. His face was a bitter challenge, a pugnacious invitation to try to fight him. In his frame, was a hardness of bone and muscle which is the heritage of those who do not succumb to the thread bareness of poverty and the anger of an empty stomach. Vito fought daily with the heavy burden of a boy determined to stay alive in an urban jungle. Just as the chemistry of the body builds up tissue and bone and blood to fight off illness, so did it fortify Vito's sullen spirit. He had trained himself not to smile or show any emotion at all. There was no need for him to speak, for in his presence one felt the electric spark of danger and violence, swift and savage, without pity or mercy; so that only a fool would mess with him. That's the image he worked to cultivate.

Vito looked at himself in the mirror. "Not bad," he thought, "no pimples or blackheads, just a little swelling above the eyes from fights and brawls he had had in school and out on the street." Nevertheless, he was pleased with what he saw, a handsome, somewhat tough looking Italian kid. "What girl wouldn't want some of this?" He thought, admiringly.

"Scram," He said to Dominic, as he entered their bedroom. "I gotta get dressed for school."

"I thought you were gonna make me breakfast?" Dominic said.

"Get it yourself, ya little brat. What am I your nigga?" Vito said, pushing his brother out of the room.

"Fuck you!" Dominic said, punching Vito in the back. "You're a jerk off!" He spat at him, running out of the room to avoid a back handed slap.

Vito opened his closet taking out a black silk bomber jacket with Black Hawks scrolled across the back in white letters. All the guys in the gang wore jackets like that. He was proud as hell of this jacket. He was accepted into the club just a month ago. Aldo Pinto, the president of the Black Hawks, presented it to him when he was made a member. The actual ceremony was just like the real mob guys did; with all the crew watching as a small cut was made on your hand. Blood was dripped on a paper picture of a saint. Then, you cupped your hands as the saint icon was set on fire. You had to hold the flaming picture in your hands until the fire burnt out. It hurt like hell, and your hands got burned, but you were supposed to show no pain or emotion. Then, you had to say this oath, *"If ever I betray my Black Hawk brothers, may my soul burn in Hell like the picture of this saint."* After this, Aldo presented him with his jacket, all the guys shook his hand and then they had a big feed. All good food from *Fiori's Italian Deli* on Adams Street, the best. Tony Messina (the founder of the Black Hawks) who was now in the military put the ceremony together. Don Franco Messina watched over the gang with a critical eye and knew every member. So, Vito was now in with real guys and he felt great about it.

"Come on," he yelled at Dominic. "I'm gonna make you eggs and toast. You put on the espresso pot so we can have coffee before we leave for school."

"I thought you told me to make it myself?" said Dom.

Vito moved the eggs around in the pan to keep them from sticking. "Just put the coffee on and shut up, I'm making the eggs for us."

"Did you put garlic in the oil?" asked Dom.

"Yeah, yeah, yeah, I don't want garlic in my eggs. I don't wanna stink all day in school. Geez, you're such a pain in the ass."

Dominic put the espresso pot on the stove, "I don't care if I stink."

"Yeah well, you're only ten years old! You're not trying to get laid. I am, and no girl wants a guy that stinks of garlic."

"Shit, you couldn't get laid in a whorehouse," Dom said, laughing.

"Where do you get that kind of talk at ten years old?" said Vito, smacking him in the head.

"Ouch, you fuck!" Dominic turned and punched his older brother in the stomach. "Next time, it'll be in your balls!"

"For crying out loud!" Vito scooped the scrambled eggs onto two plates. "Look, you little jerk off! Mom is working late tonight, so

15

here's ten dollars. Go get something at the deli for dinner when you get home from school."

"Won't you be coming home?" Dom asked.

"None of your business."

"I was only asking you. I'm always alone in this place."

"So, watch T.V. or something. What am I supposed to entertain you? I got other shit to do. So, do you want the ten bucks or not?"

Dominic stuck out his hand. "Give it to me."

They finished their breakfast. Vito told Dominic to leave for school while he cleaned the dishes. As soon as he left, Vito rinsed the dishes, dried them putting them away in the cabinet. The apartment was becoming seedy looking; with his mother working so many hours, there was no one to clean the place. The windows hadn't been washed in months and the furniture was full of dust. He looked out the window at a rusted fire escape and an alleyway littered with broken bottles and trash. Yeah, the place sure was a dump. If only his father hadn't gone to jail for bookmaking, his mother wouldn't have to work overtime. Maybe, if his father got his job back at the shipyard, they could move and get out of this shit hole. Ah well, what was the use of thinking about it. He looked at the clock. It was already eight thirty and school had started at eight. Who gave a shit about school anyway? He went into his room, opened the top drawer of his dresser taking out a metal box. He opened the lock with a key removing three marijuana joints, and his pistol. He took out six 22. caliber shells, flipped open the barrel inserting the bullets. He hefted the gun in his hand and put the pistol in the right front pocket of his pants. He looked at himself in the mirror, combed his hair one last time and left the apartment. As he walked down the dark narrow steps of the tenement, he felt as he always did; that he was in a prison and was walking to his freedom. He passed through the dirty hallway and the neighboring apartment doors with their chipped paint and dingy opaque glass panels. He ducked as he passed under the electric light fixtures which hung awry and looked as if they might fall at any moment from the ceiling. It was good to get out on the street and into the sunlight. He hurried up to the corner of Fourth and Monroe because he saw two of the Hawks there. One was Blackie Carrozza. His real name was Phillipo but because his hair was jet black the gang called him Blackie. He liked the name, it sounded tough. The other was Mikey Sabatelli. Both were fellow Black Hawks.

"Going to school today?" Mikey asked Vito.

Vito looked over at Blackie. "No I'm not going to school."

"Want to go to the movies?" Blackie replied. "They got a good movie at the Paramount theater. We could sneak in if Sam the manager isn't on his game. If he catches us sneaking in, he'll boot us right out on our asses."

"Yeah, okay," said Vito, "We haven't cut school for a couple of days."

Mikey shook his head. "I don't know why we're even wasting our time in school? We should just get our working papers and get a job before the Army grabs us and sends us to Viet Nam like they did with Tony Messina. I hear he's in the thick of it over there."

"Yeah, I'd like to quit but my parents want me to get my diploma," said Blackie. "Now, they're even talking about me going to college."

"College?" Mikey punched him in the shoulder. "They gotta be batty! College? What the hell are you gonna do there? That college shit's for the birds! Listen, if we get hooked up with Joey Messina we'll be set for life, made men with money coming in like water. Fuck college, that shit's for saps. Look at Aldo Pinto, with Tony in the military, Aldo is Joey Messina's main guy with the Hawks. Look, Aldo just bought himself a brand new 66 Chevy Impala. What a sweet ride that is! How would ya like to be cruising around in one of those jobs, huh, how 'bout that?"

"Yeah, that would be nice." said Vito.

"Me too," nodded Blackie.

"We'll just stick with the Hawks and just maybe the Messina family will take notice. Then we're talkin' big time my friends, big time cash, cars and broads, the works! College my ass!"

Vito and Blackie nodded in the affirmative. "Oh, by the way," said Vito, "I picked up some counterfeit money from Jo-Jo Manetti; it's an easy way to pick up some fast cash, are you guys in?"

"Does the money look good?" asked Blackie.

"Hell, the bills look so real you can't tell the difference and he asks twenty bucks for a hundred, ya can't loose."

"Where can we pass them?" asked Mikey.

Vito laughed, "Anywhere! The bills are good. That's how I'm making scratch these days. Just don't pass them in our neighborhood because eventually somebody will get wise and then, well, it's a federal pinch. Just take a bus into Manhattan and buy clothes, smokes and a lot of other shit. Hand them a twenty and the change is yours. It's a cinch." Vito took out a roll of bills and handed Mikey and Blackie a couple of twenties each. "Here, these are on me, see what you can do with them. If you want anymore, let me know and I'll talk to Jo-Jo for you."

"Thanks," Blackie said.

"Yeah, thanks a lot," reiterated Mikey. "You're a stand up guy, Vito, a real Hawk."

Chapter 3

Vito and Blackie stood in front of the Paramount Theater waiting for it to open for the mid-morning show. They decided that this was a lot more fun then sitting in class at Hoboken High School. School was a bunch of bullshit anyway. Blackie agreed, but what could you do when your old man and old lady insisted that you get an education?

Vito winked at some hot looking girls passing by, obviously cutting school themselves. The girls turned around motioning to Vito and Blackie to come along with them.

"Don't follow them," said Blackie, as Vito started to follow them. "We can pick them up just as easy in the show. This way we don't got to pay for their tickets."

"But they're hot pieces," said Vito.

"The hell with that," said Blackie, lighting a cigarette and taking a long drag. "You can't see them in the dark anyway."

"You cheap fuck, I just gave you a couple of knock off twenties, be a sport man."

"Yeah, you're right. Let's get them."

For three and a half hours they sat in the balcony of the Paramount theater necking with two high school girls who were also cutting school that day. First, Vito made out with one of the girls, then swapped with Blackie. He liked Blackie's girl better. She didn't kiss as wet and she smelled cleaner than the first one he had. Also, she let him feel her up, which was a plus.

"Let me call you sometime?" Vito asked her. "Will you meet me?"

"Sure," she said, "We can go dancing."

"That sounds great." Vito's hand slipped into her blouse caressing her soft breasts.

She smiled and said, "I like that. After we go dancing, what can we do?"

Vito kissed her lips while touching her. "We can go eat at a nice restaurant." He slipped his hand between her legs.

She stiffened up. "No, no, I don't go that far," she said, pouting her lips, "Not yet, anyway," pushing his hand away.

Vito stared at her intently, "Look babe, I'll be straight with you right off the bat. I don't like a tease, and I'm sure not going home with blue balls, understand?"

"I'm not a tease," she said, "Now, be a nice guy and let me watch the movie."

"Just one more kiss?" Vito moved in again. "I really like you," he said, kissing and pressing himself against her.

The girl slid low in her seat and placed her head on Vito's shoulder. "I like you, too." She placed his hand on her breast again and held it. "Now, let's watch the movie."

It was half-past one when they walked out of the theater and onto the street, the bright warm sun making them blink. As they stood in front of the theater, Vito could see the girl he had been making out with in the light of day. He was glad that he had swapped with Blackie. Her name was Angela. She was a dark haired, dark eyed Italian girl about sixteen and wore high heeled shoes. The hem of her black skirt was just above her knees. She had nice legs and she knew it. She wore a red blouse open at the collar showing just enough cleavage. Her face was perfectly pretty and Vito thought that she looked like the actress Natalie Wood. He could feel himself getting excited just thinking what it would be like to really be alone with her. When she laughed her teeth were white and even. Her makeup was put on just right, not too heavy, just enough to enhance her natural beauty. She was a beautiful girl, smooth and confident in her appearance.

"Come over here," Vito said, pulling her to him and kissing her firmly on the lips, not to hard and not too soft, just enough to let her know that he was in charge of the situation. She liked his confidence and mastery, she kissed him back. "I want your phone number," he said.

Angela smiled, "I'll give it to you when we get something to eat."

"Sure," Vito smiled back at her, then turning to Blackie said, "Hey, let's take the girls for lunch, waddaya say?"

"Okay," said Blackie," let's go."

Vito was glad that he had a girl to hang out with while he was cutting school. Usually when he cut school after he got out of the movies there wasn't anything to do. If he went down to the club no one was there, if he hung out on the corner no one was there, unless a bunch of the guys cut school on the same day. But this was cool, hanging out with a hot piece and having lunch at Schaffer's Diner. Time passed so fast that it was past four o'clock when they left the girls, after promising to call them so they could make a date to see them the next day.

"Yeah"…,Vito smacked Blackie on the back, "I'm sure gonna have a good time with Angela tomorrow."

"I shouldn't have swapped with you," said Blackie. "Your girl, Angela, is better looking than mine. But I don't care, I think Anna is pretty, but not as hot as Angela. But I don't care, Vito, 'cause you always get the hottest babes."

"Knock it off," said Vito, embarrassed.

"Aw, I don't give a shit," Blackie said. "They're both sexy as hell. I'm gonna get my old man's car for tomorrow, then we'll take them to my house and try to bang 'em."

"What about your parents?"

"They're in Italy. My Nonna died. They had to go to the funeral and all that stuff."

"They left the car?"

"Yeah, what were they gonna do, take it to Sicily with them?" Blackie laughed.

"Great man, you're cool man, a really cool guy," Vito said, appreciatively. "One cool guy!"

"Yeah," Blackie pinched Vito's cheek, "Maybe ya wanna kiss me?"

Vito pulled away. "Knock it off, ya fag. Let's get going. I wanna go home and check on my kid brother. I gotta make sure the little prick don't burn the place down. Then I'll meet you on the corner at six."

"Na, six is no good. I gotta eat then shower and get dressed. I'll meet you at the club at eight, okay?"

As soon as Vito turned the corner from Fourth Street onto Monroe, there it was. That dirty, stinking block. The ugly grey and green tenements, veritable tombstones of poverty and smoldering violence and unrest. They were crowded close together and rose straight up on both sides of the street to shut out all but a narrow view of the sky. It was as if nothing bright would ever shine on Monroe Street. Each tenement had a rusted iron fence against which rested dented garbage cans and paper bags of trash piled against the cans. Women and children flanked the entrances of the tenements, cursing and shouting in Southern Italian dialect.

When Vito saw his little brother, Dominic, in an alleyway shooting craps with some other kids, he grabbed him by the arm and pulled him onto the sidewalk. "What the hell are ya doing?!" He yelled, shaking Dom by the shoulder.

"Get your hands off me!" Dominic yelled back, pulling away. "You're not my boss!"

"You're Goddamn right I'm your boss, you little shit. And where the hell did you get the cash to shoot craps with?"

"I just got it, that's all. It's none a ya business! You're not Dad or Mom!" Dominic spit the words out, venomously. "So, let go of me and leave me alone!"

"That's the ten dollars I gave you this morning to buy yourself dinner, isn't it?"

"Yeah, so what?!"

Vito softened, "Dominic, that money was for you to get yourself something nice to eat, not lose it playing craps in a friggin alleyway. You're only ten years old, and I'm your big brother. Mom and Dad ain't here so I'm supposed to look after you. How much do you have left?"

"I got more than ten dollars," Dom said. "I was winning when you pulled me away. I got twenty five bucks now, and I would have more if you left me alone, you jerk!"

"Twenty five dollars? You got twenty five bucks? Then give me back the ten I gave you."

"Fuck you, Vito, that ten you gave me was a fugazee[6] anyway and you know it. Wadda think, I'm stupid? Dom laughed, "I might only be ten but I wasn't born yesterday."

Vito smiled and put his arm around his brother. "Come on kid, let's spend some of that money and get a good meal at Romano's Restaurant."

Dominic nodded his head hugging Vito around the waist. "Okay, let's eat. Can I have meatballs and ravioli?"

---

6   Fugezee: A fake.

"Yeah, and cannoli for dessert with some expresso, okay, buddy?"

"Okay, by me," said Dominic, jumping up and down. They walked to the restaurant laughing and pushing each other down the sidewalk. "Good thing I played craps, right?"

"Yeah, I guess so," said Vito, sighing. "But maybe instead of doing that, next time you can go over to Saint Ann's Church Center and play basketball or something with Father Joe. He's a good guy and he'll watch out for you until I get home."

At the restaurant, Vito looked quizzically at his brother. He wished that Dominic didn't make him feel like such a heel. It wasn't his fault that his father was in the can and his mother had to work double shifts to put some food on the table and pay the rent. If his mother got a dollar sixty an hour for piece work in a sewing shop, it wasn't a lot. But when she got into overtime and started to get two dollars and sixty cents an hour, that was real money. Now, Dom was hanging out on the streets with no supervision. With their parents not being home, Vito felt that it was damn inconsiderate of the kid. But then he figured, he was only ten and didn't know any better. He just didn't want him to get hurt or worse while he was supposed to look out for him.

"Listen, Dom, you gotta stop hanging out on the streets," he told him. "I know it's tough on you, and even on me with you being alone so much. But if Mom don't make the dough, who knows what will happen to us? We can't live on the street, ya know." He shrugged his shoulders, "After Pop gets out of the can maybe we can be a family again. Maybe we can move into a nicer place."

"I don't want to move, I like it just fine where we live now. I'm starting to get known on the street and I got friends."

"What?!" Vito started up in his chair. "You're starting to get known on the street?! You're ten fucking years old! What the hell are you doing that you're getting known on the block?! Finish your cannoli and let's go home! When we get back to the apartment, just do your homework and go to bed. I gotta go out tonight."

"Did you do your homework?" Dominic asked.

"Never you mind what I do; just do your homework and go to bed."

"Sometimes I get scared when I'm alone," said Dominic.

"Scared? I thought you were a tough guy, known on the streets and all. So, what the hell are you scared of?"

"I don't know, I just get scared. Sometimes, I think that idiot crazy Joey Pazzo is gonna come in the window from the fire escape and hurt me. He scares the shit outta me. Vito, you should kick his ass."

Vito shook his head. "When we get back, just do your homework and go to bed. Like I said, I'm going out tonight."

Laurie Petolla, a fifteen year old piece of ass, was hanging around their stoop when Vito said goodnight to Dominic. He could tell by the way she looked at him that she would have given anything if he'd invite her to the Black Hawks Club. As he walked down Monroe Street, he could feel her eyes upon him. He consciously swaggered, for he was a Black Hawk and that meant that he was on top of the world.

The Black Hawks had a clubroom on Seventh and Adams Street. Above the entrance, a black and yellow sign read 'Black Hawks'. To the right of the entrance door was a little room that the guys used as a coat room. The main room had a polished wood floor. It was furnished with furniture stolen from freight trains stopped along the railroad tracks behind the Marshall Drive Projects. It was decorated with sofas, lounge chairs, some end tables loaded with ash trays, and floor lamps. The Hawks had an operation that broke open freight cars and stole whatever was inside. The boxcars held mostly furnishings which was great for their clubroom. Picture frames held prints of landscapes with posters of Italy dotted the walls. A stereo system with speakers was indented into the ceiling so that music could be played when the Black Hawks held a dance. At the far end of the room, was another door which led to a kitchen and a bathroom. Another door led to a room with two beds and end tables for times when one of the guys had a girl he wanted to be intimate with.

On any night there would be some of the guys in the club room with their girlfriends listening to music or making out. A group would be standing out front on the sidewalk trying to pick up girls who would regularly walk the streets of the neighborhood looking to meet guys and dance. The Black Hawks were always lucky with the girls because they had a reputation for being a sharp bunch of guys. A string of girls came around every night to dance and make out. The Hawks always had money in their pockets, It was a mortal sin to be considered a cheap skate, especially where girls were concerned. The Black Hawks had three rules which they had to observe: they had to pay their dues promptly, they had to be ready to fight for one another at any given time, and they had to always carry a gun. Backing down from any confrontation was considered to be the worst dishonor. It was reprimanded by a vicious beating from fellow Black Hawk members and you could be banned from the club. They also had to dress sharply at all times. Sloppy, wrinkled clothes were frowned upon. Italian knit shirts and matching color pants with silk socks and city shoes were the uniform of the day. They were always expected to be clean shaven and have a sharp haircut. Nice gold jewelry, I.D. bracelets, gold chains and pinky rings were encouraged if not by word then by example. Each of the Hawks was an expert at minding his own business; no one muscled in on another guys action. The Black Hawks was the club to belong to and all the guys knew it.

They realized it most when the Hawks threw a party. Then there was a band, guests from other gangs, maybe a real mobster from the Messina family and his date, and lots of babes who flocked to any party the Hawks threw. The lights were dim and private, but there was never any rough stuff. Any guy who got out of line or started a fight was thrown out and got his ass kicked .

Every two weeks, there was a meeting night with only members allowed. A case of beer was brought in as well as catered food from Fiore's Italian Deli. The members would sit around and discuss how they could make money for the club and for themselves. They had a shoplifting crew that took two vans to small towns in South Jersey. They would stake out clothing stores on the avenues. The van would pull up in front of the store, two guys would run in and grab as many leather jackets, or shirts or whatever they could easily grab in a half a minute, run out to the van and drive off. Then, the clothing would be sold in a small store in Union City. Tony Messina originally set this system up and it continued to be a money maker for the Black Hawks. Then there was the liquor store robberies and the box car break ins. Once in awhile, the crew would go into Jersey City at night and knock the heads off of parking meters grabbing the change therein. So, basically, the meeting nights were a meeting of the minds of who to rob next. Selling marijuana was something that was becoming a big money maker for the Hawks. Aldo Pinto had a connection in Greenwich Viallage who brought in pounds that were cut up and weighed on meeting nights. It was then sold by the ounce to guys who liked to partake of the forbidden weed.

As Vito walked along Adam's Street, he could see the sign in front of the clubroom inviting him. He walked up, knocking on the door in code, the door opened slightly.

"It's me, Vito," he whispered.

"Come in", Joey Pazzo said. "We got some whore inside and we're lining up on her."

"Who is she?" Asked Vito.

"That Spic broad from Jackson Street, Monica Sosa. She's taking us all on." Joey licked his lips, lustfully, "Are you in?"

"No fucking way am I lining up on a broad after everybody had their dick in her. No friggin way, that's disgusting!"

"Have it your way," said Joey, "but I'm going in."

"Yeah, it figures he would," thought Vito, "crazy bastard that he is." Vito walked over to one of the lounge chairs flopping into the cushion. He took a reefer joint out of his cigarette case and lit it. No one was doing much, the guys were going in and out of the room where the Puerto Rican girl was taking them on one by one. Vito wished he hadn't come down to the club. Maybe, he should have stayed home with his little brother, Dominic, and watched T.V. with him. The poor kid was always alone. Now, he was hanging out in alleyways playing craps with the other mutts on the block. What the hell did he expect anyway? What else was the kid supposed to do?

Blackie came out of the room, zippering up his pants.

"How was she?" asked Vito.

"She was okay, she blew me that's all. I wouldn't bone her. Who the hell knows where that spic has been."

"Well, if she's taking guys on line, something's got to be wrong with her in the head, ya know?" Vito said, tapping his temple.

"Oh, Mr. Big Shot is so fussy," said Joey Pazzo, butting in.

Vito took a long drag on the reefer, held it in, then let the smoke out slowly. "Get the fuck away from me!" He said to Joey.

Joey spit on the floor in front of him, "*Cornude*" [7]he scowled, staring hatefully at Vito. "Hey guys," he said, "How about we all give this spic broad a beating, smack her around a little?"

Anthony Carbone, who was sitting in one of the lounge chairs said, "What are you, a sick fuck, Joey?! Why the hell would we want to beat her up?!"

"No, honest," Joey insisted. "It'll be really good. We'll really smack her around and then bang her!"

"Suppose she gets some Latin Kings to come down from Jersey City to fuck us up?" Anthony asked him.

"Fuhgettaboutit." Joey walked toward him, his hands shaking with excitement. "Those Spics step foot on our block and we'll blast them." He took out his revolver and aimed it at the door. "We'll blast those Spics to hell. Come on, let's smack her around real good, then fuck the shit outta her!" Little drops of saliva drooled down his chin as he described what he would do to her.

The boys sat tensely in their chairs listening as Joey went on and on with his sadistic rant. They knew that Joey Pazzo was a sicko, but he was also a dangerous guy to cross or insult and all too ready to pull his gun on a guy or even stab him. In fact, some of the boys weren't too crazy about having Joey in the Hawks because he acted too nutty to suit them. However, he was good in a pinch, or as a backup when there was a rumble with another gang. Joey walked with a slight stooping of his strong shoulders. His straight black hair grew out of a thick massive skull. His jaw protruded into an anvil like square, setting off a dull, stupid face. His eyes mirrored his ignorance and bewilderment of a world he did not fully understand. The constant torment, jeers and insults he received as a child, being called stupid and a retard; had made Joey dangerous, and within him was a smoldering hate that changed him from a dull boy into a dangerous, maniacal street fighter. But the idea of abusing this girl was nuts even for Joey, and now the boys waited for Big Aldo Pinto, the club president, to step in.

---

7   Son of a bitch!

"So how about it Aldo?" asked Anthony.

"Fuck no, and double no!" Said Aldo, looking at Joey while shaking his head. "We're not smacking a girl around and that's final!" Aldo was a big, six foot, 200 lb. slugger who kept Joey Pazzo and the rest of the guys in line with the sheer force of his will. The Black Hawk gang were all a bunch of tough nuts to crack, so Aldo Pinto had to be tougher. With fists like hammers, he resembled a young Rocky Marciano, no one messed with him. It was said that Don Franco Messina had his eye on Aldo as a future collector and enforcer.

Just then the door of the bedroom opened and one of the guys told Joey that it was his turn to go in. Joey giggled fiendishly, while making slugging motions with his fists.

"You better not hurt that girl!" Aldo scolded Joey.

"Okay," Joey said, hanging his head stupidly as he entered the room.

"Who hasn't gone in the room?" Aldo asked.

"You, Vito?"

The reefer was making Vito feel dreamy. "Nah, I don't wanna go," said Vito.

"Why?" Blackie asked him.

"I just don't want to!"

"Vito's stoned!" Blackie said.

"All right," Aldo spoke decisively. "After Joey gets through in there, we'll let her go. We'll give her a few bucks and send her back to the Jackson Street Projects."

"Yeah," Anthony laughed, "send her back to her Spic friends and tell them that the guineas had a time with her Latina ass!"

As she opened the door coming out into the clubroom, she blinked. She was only about sixteen or seventeen years old, the most. She was pretty, dark skinned, brown eyed, with high breasts and a small waist. She wore a short skirt and high heels. Her blouse was torn as were her pantyhose covering young shapely legs. She looked a mess, with her hair disheveled, her lipstick and make up smeared across her young face. Already, she showed signs of physical decay as glassy dilated eyes and needle marks belied drug addiction which if not abated would eventually kill her.

"Well, is everybody happy?" She said smiling, trying to look pretty.

"You were alright," Blackie said.

She looked at Aldo, "Can I have some money? I'm starting to feel sick. I need a fix and I don't have any money."

Aldo looked over at Anthony and said. "Go get some cash out of the box and give her a twenty."

"Wait!" Said Joey Pazzo, "Why give this Spic bitch anything? She should pay us for the privilege of getting laid by Italians."

Anthony came back and handed the girl a twenty dollar bill. "Thanks," she said, starting to leave. She stopped as she saw Joey Pazzo push one of the large arm chairs in front of the door sitting down in it. "Let me out!" her voice became nervous and shrill.

"When you give us back our money," Joey said.

"Get out of my way!" She said, looking as if she were going to cry. Joey put his foot in the middle of her stomach kicking her into the middle of the room. As she reeled backward on her high heels, she fell on her back, her skirt above her thighs.

None of the boys spoke as she sat on the floor sobbing. "Please, let me go home," she wept.

"You gotta give us our money back and blow me again," said Joey, shaking with excitement.

"You'll get yours!" She screamed with fright and fury, "I'm gonna get the Kings on you, you ginzo bastards!"

"Tell them!" Joey screamed in her face, "Tell those Spic pussies to come here, tell them, I dare ya!" He pulled his revolver out of his pocket. "Tell your Spic relatives to come onto our turf, just tell them, I fucking dare ya!" Joey stood up walking towards her menacingly. She backed away from him toward one end of the room, her eyes filled with fright, looking down the barrel of Joey's revolver.

Suddenly, a hard slap across Joey's face sent him reeling into the wall. Aldo stood there seething, as he slapped Joey a second and a third time. Joey dropped his gun and stood leaning against the wall shaking. Aldo grabbed him by the hair spitting full in his face. He then twisted his hair until he fell to his knees. Aldo pulled out his pistol shoving it into Joey's mouth. "You cowardly scumbag! You hit a girl in my club?! You low life piece of shit! I ought to take this gun and blow your brains out right here in front of everyone!"

Aldo looked over at the girl saying, "Go home, go on get outta here." She put her head down and ran out of the door onto the street. Joey stared wide-eyed as Aldo Pinto pressed the barrel of the gun harder into his mouth. Aldo then pushed him aside, disgustedly.

Vito stared at the ceiling trying not to be part of what was going on. The whole thing made him sick. Joey Pazzo, kicking the young girl and pulling his piece on her, while she sat limply in the middle of the floor trying to cover herself while she wept. It was horrible, it just sucked period! Not at all something an Italian would do to a young girl. But that's what came from hanging out with a crazy bastard like Joey.

Vito continued to stare at the ceiling. "I think we're a bunch of assholes," he said.

"It wasn't my idea," said Blackie.

"Well?" Aldo's voice was rigid and hard, and his eyes glowed. I'm gonna give you all another minute to forget what happened here. If you don't, you're all gonna get a beating! And you!" He said, looking down at Joey. "If you ever pull a stunt like that again in this club, these guys here will be mopping your brains off the floor, if you have any brains in that stupid head of yours!" He turned walking into the backroom and slammed the door behind him.

"Jeez," said Joey, "what the hell did I do?"

Vito lit a third joint and puffed hard on the reefer. It took three of them now to make him feel really high. As he took the first couple of drags on the weed, the comedy of the episode struck him and he began to laugh wildly, stamping his feet and punching the arm of the lounge chair. Soon, some of the other boys began to laugh, partly at him and partly at the release of tension. The clubroom rocked with laughter as Joey Pazzo sat at a card table with his head in his hands complaining how everyone always blamed him when he did nothing wrong. In his stupid, vicious and violent way, Joey was obscenely funny, and the boys were limp from laughing. This was really some night.

Blackie looked at his wrist watch and saw that it was past eleven. "You coming?" he asked Vito as he stood up. "We're goin' to get somethin' to eat, anybody comin'?"

"I'll go wit' ya," Joey Pazzo shouted.

"Aw, shit," Vito muttered. "I've had enough of that idiot for one night."

Vito left the clubroom with Blackie, Joey, Anthony, Aldo, and Torro Tedesco. On the corner of First and Grand Streets, they stopped in "Leo's" for pizza and mussels. They listened to Frank Sinatra on the jukebox, the only singing artist that Leo had on the box except for Jimmy Roselli, a local Italian singer. They were all underage for drinking at the bar but they were Black Hawks and this was downtown Hoboken where cash was better than an I.D.

They left the bar after midnight, all drunk and stupid. Vito was coming down from his marijuana high and was feeling kind of

33

cranky. Joey Pazzo was yelling and running his mouth about how he was gonna kill some spics if he saw them walking on Black Hawk turf. He was sparring, throwing punches and waving around his switchblade knife; no one could shut him up. Vito wondered why Joey was even a Black Hawk; he was such an idiot. But then he remembered that Joey Pazzo was one of the best guys they had when they got into a fight. He was a scary bastard that was for sure. He got thrown out of high school and put into Jamesburg Reformatory for three years for trying to rape a Puerto Rican girl. He then stabbed her brother for trying to defend her. Yeah, Joey Pazzo surely lived up to his name.[8]

The night air was clearing Vito's head. He was starting to feel better. As they walked down Jefferson Street, three guys passed them on the sidewalk. Vito turned punching one of them in the back of the head because, as they passed, he recognized them as being Spics from the Jackson Street Projects. They wore red silk jackets with "Alkies" scrawled across the back. They wore pointed roach killer shoes and multicolored Santeria beads around their necks. The boy Vito slugged stumbled forward hitting the ground on his knees. Vito approached him coldly staring him in the eyes.

"Watcha hit me for?" asked the Puerto Rican kid, while his friends started circling Vito.

"I don't like you, that's why! I don't like spics in my neighborhood!" Vito's face twitched, his hand in his pocket holding his revolver.

"And we don't like fucking guineas either!" One of the other Puerto Ricans said to Vito.

"Shut your fucking mouth!' Aldo Pinto advised the stranger, "No one asked you anything, you filthy spic! Do you know where you're at right now? You cockroaches fucked up!"

---

8   Pazzo means "Crazy" in Italian

Joey Pazzo pushed his way in between, "Where're you from? What block you spics from?"

"Central Ave. in Jersey City."

"Bullshit!" yelled Joey. "You guys got "Alki" Jackets on! You're from the Jackson Street Projects trying to say you're from Central Ave.. They're trying to make us think they're "Latin Kings" to save their asses."

"So, what makes you guineas think your shit don't stink?" The kid who had been punched said. Then he realized that he had made a big mistake and backed away. The Puerto Ricans were only three against five. Torro Tedesco, built like a fireplug with a strong jaw that set off the thickness of his cruel smile, looked like the kind of slugger who could take on two or three guys all by himself. And the guy who kept jumping and bopping around with an open switch-blade in his hand looked like he was totally nuts and a slasher.

"We don't want no problems, man!" he motioned to his friends to start walking. But Torro and Anthony blocked the sidewalk.

"Hold on there, Chico," Anthony said. "What the hell are you guys doing on Grand Street anyway? You know this is Black Hawk turf!"

"Man, we just coming from Washington Street. We saw a movie at the Paramount and we're going home. We don't want no beef, just going home."

"How the hell do we know?!" Vito asked, aggressively. "Maybe you're the guys who spray painted 'Alkies' all over Saint Ann's Church last week."

"Man, we didn't do shit! Now, get out of our way!" the Puerto Rican said. There was silence while the two groups stared each other down.

"You know you spics are a fucking bunch of shitbags," Torro said. "I got a brother in the Marines. He was wounded over in Nam and is still in the hospital. How do you think he'd feel about a bunch of dirty spics spraying up our Church?"

"Man, I told you, we didn't do shit to your Church!" The second Puerto Rican kid tried to edge away, but Joey blocked him.

"That's what you say," Blackie spat angrily. "I think you guys did it! What other reason would you be in this neighborhood?!"

"Man, I told you, we were at the Paramount watching a fucking movie, man! We cut across town to get home faster. Now, get the fuck out of the way, man!" The Puerto Rican kid tried to push past Torro with a strong shove. Torro hit him with a short jab to the stomach that knocked the wind out of him. He curled forward while Torro landed an uppercut to the kid's face. He was knocked out cold before he even hit the sidewalk.

That was the signal. Vito went for the kid he had punched in the head and kicked him between the legs. The kid buckled over falling to his knees while holding his groin. Vito's knee caught him in the chin. His eyes rolled in back of his head and he was done. Then, Blackie kicked him in the face smashing out his teeth. Now, the gang turned on the other Puerto Rican. Joey ran at him like a crazy man while swinging his knife, as the boy tried to defend himself. The blade cut into the boys face slicing open his right cheek; as the blood spit out like a fountain. The boy screamed as he ran down the street holding his lacerated face.

"You see, you see, you spic bastards!" Joey Pazzo panted. "This is what happens when you fuck with Italians! Now, I'm gonna finish you!" Joey ran down the street chasing the wounded Puerto Rican. The rest of the Black Hawks ran after him.

"You stupid son of a bitch!" Aldo yelled after Joey, "What did you have to cut him for?!"

"Because he's a spic and he spray painted our Church!"

"Aw, shut up!" Aldo said, and saved his breath for running. They ran a couple of blocks turning down Fourth Street towards Adams Street. Joey Pazzo was walking ahead of everyone laughing to himself. Every once in awhile he would do a little dance or jump over a fire hydrant. Vito turned away from him in disgust. "What a fucking idiot!" He thought, watching Joey acting like a fool.

"Man, oh man," Joey said. "We sure had a great time tonight. We got laid by a spic, then beat up some spics, and I cut the shit out of one. Man, oh man, did you see him bleed?" He started laughing and singing some Italian song. "We shouldn't have let that spic girl leave with the twenty dollars. Fuck her! We should have kicked her around and threw her out on her ass; fucking spic whore, drug addict!"

Vito scowled at him. "Man, can't you stop talking?! All you do is run your mouth! Shut the fuck up!"

"You shut the fuck up man! I'm not talking to you! ho the hell do you think you are, anyway?!" Joey blustered.

Suddenly, Vito hit him flush in the mouth, knocking him to the sidewalk. Joey was dazed and laid on the ground shaking his head. Before he could get up, Vito dealt him another smashing blow to the side of the head. As he fell prone, Vito kicked him twice in the kidneys. Joey was done.

"That," Vito said, "was for giving my little brother the finger and saying that you screwed my mother!"

"Did he do that?" Aldo asked him, seriously.

"Yeah, the crazy bastard! This morning my little brother was looking out the window, and from across the alley, Joey gave him the finger and said, *Tu madre e una putana!*" I can't let him get away with that shit! He shouldn't even be a Black Hawk! He's got no friggin class! He's a goddamn dirt bag!"

As Anthony helped Joey to his feet, Vito turned to him. "I'm warning you!" he spat at Joey. "If you ever even look at my little brother again, they're gonna be finding your body parts all over the state of New Jersey!"

Joey stood up, enraged. "You hit me when I wasn't looking, you piece of shit! I oughta slice you up right now!" He screamed, pulling out his stiletto.

"Just try it, you fucking retard!" Vito said, getting into a fighting stance while reaching for his pistol. But Blackie grabbed him from behind dragging him away, as Aldo held back Joey.

"You don't fuck with anybody in my family!" Vito growled, furiously. "I'll ruin you, you son of a bitch!!"

"Yeah, make a move scumbag!" Joey growled, as Aldo pulled him down the street trying to calm him.

Vito pulled away from Blackie and walked down Fourth Street to Monroe Street towards his tenement house. He felt lousy. It was two in the morning and his head hurt. His whole body ached as he walked in solitude on the deserted streets. He didn't know how he was going to get up in the morning. He knew that Dominic was going to wake him up in the morning to go to school.

The hallway was dark and the smell of mildew was more pronounced since the weather was getting warmer. Wearily, he climbed the stairs to the third floor of the tenement house. He opened the door of the apartment with his key, took off his shoes, quietly shutting the door. He stopped to listen to his little brother breathing. He took the pistol from his jacket pocket, putting it in the dresser drawer where it would be safe until morning.

Vito walked over to his brother gently shaking him.

"V?" Dominic asked sleepily, as he looked at his older brother.

"Listen, kid," Vito said, "That lunatic, Joey, won't ever bother you again, I just kicked his ass and warned him never to bother anyone in our family again."

"Really?" Dom said, sitting up. "Really, that's good Vito. Wow, you really kicked his ass?"

"Yep, I smacked the shit outta him. The *jerdrool*[9] didn't have a chance. So, you don't have to worry about him anymore," said Vito, rubbing his brother's head. "Did Momma come home?"

"Yeah, she got home about eleven o'clock and went right to bed. She was too tired to even talk to me. But that's okay, I guess she was really tired from working that double shift."

"I guess she was," said Vito, sadly. "Now, you just go back to sleep and don't worry about nothing 'cause I'm here, okay?"

"Okay!" said Dominic, smiling. He turned over, hugging his pillow and went back to sleep.

Vito felt like a creep leaving his brother all alone every night. He had to be less selfish. He promised himself that he would be more of a big brother to Dom. He started to get into bed and stopped. He went back into the kitchen, turned on the light, and found a note, a ten dollar bill and some change on the table. That meant that his mother would be working late again tomorrow. "Poor Dom," he said, he felt sorry for the kid, he was always alone.

---

9   A cucumber or in Italian American street lingo a Jerk.

Chapter 4

Vito had no intention of going to school Monday morning. He had plans with Blackie who promised to use his father's car to take the girls they met at the Paramount theater out for the day. Vito was excited thinking of Angela and how hot she was. He couldn't wait to get alone with her and see how far he could get. As he descended the tenement steps, he saw Blackie sitting behind the wheel of his father's 1964 Rambler Classic Convertible, smiling and very pleased with the entire situation. To Vito the car was an escape, a call to freedom from the dull, grimy streets of the neighborhood. The car's tank was filled with gas purchased with the counterfeit currency Vito had provided.

They had a great time driving up to Castle Point, hanging out in Elysian Field lying in the grass trying to catch an early tan. They were able to flirt with a couple of good looking girls from the town houses on Hudson Street. The girls were impressed with their tough guy attitude and asked Vito and Blackie to call them. These girls from Castle Point with their designer clothes and manicured nails had class and assurance. Vito told Blackie that he should tone it down when he talked to them, to not be so aggressive. Blackie laughed and told him, "Remember what Frank Sinatra said in the movie "Pal Joey?" You treat a lady like a tramp and a tramp like a lady, if you wanna score."

"Yeah," laughed Vito, "a couple of stiff drinks and some reefer and they'll all put out for ya."

Blackie nodded, "And if they won't smoke the bud, just slip a couple of aspirins in with their drink and they're jelly in your hands."

Vito figured that he had at least some morals and getting a girl high in order to take advantage of her was something that he felt uncomfortable with. But a guy couldn't be weak about stuff like that because if he didn't take the opportunity, somebody else would. And what the hell, smoking pot wasn't that bad, a lot of guys were snorting heroine or even shooting up. So, smoking reefer was just kinda like drinking and he liked it better than getting drunk. Booze made you do stupid shit, pot made you mellow. But no matter what it was, nothing was going to get so much of a hold on him that he was out of control; like these stupid Irish guys, getting drunk and acting like a bunch of slobs, tripping all over themselves and slurring their words. Italian men always had to be in control of themselves, that was manhood.

"Well, we should call the girls soon," said Blackie.

"Yeah," nodded Vito, "where will we take them?"

"We'll bring them over to my place. Nobody's there since my parents are in Sicily."

"Great idea," said Vito, slapping him on the back. "Can we use their bedroom?"

"Get the fuck outta here, you *cafone*[10] your not gonna screw on my mom's bed! Jeez, not with all the statues of the Saints in the room!"

"Really?" started Vito, "You guys got Saints all over the house, too?"

---

10 *Cafone*, Italian American slang for slob.

"Shit, I think my mothers got every Saint in Heaven on every piece of furniture in the place."

"And those votive candles?" Laughed Vito.

"Yeah, yeah, yeah," nodded Blackie, "and plastic seat covers on all the chairs and on the couch."

"Shit, my place too, like they're gonna use the furniture for ever." Vito and Blackie were laughing so hard that they didn't see six members of the 'Alkies' mulling around the car. When Blackie saw them he yelled, "Hey, get the fuck off the car, man!"

"Fuck you, guido!" The Puerto Rican yelled back. Blackie and Vito ran over to the car confronting the 'Alkie' gang members.

"I said get off my car, you dirty spic bastards!" Blackie roared at them.

"Oh, big tough Black Hawk," said one of the Alkies. "There's six of us and only two of you guinea *putos*." The other night you guys jumped three of our guys when you outnumbered them. So now, you *maricons*[11] are gonna find out where you're living." They started circling. laughing and taunting, "You *putos* not so tough now, eh? Now, you gonna see Rican justice, now you gonna see."

Just then a squad car pulled up. Two police officers got out and walked up to the group. "What are you gang bangers doing up here in Castle Point?" They asked. The teenagers just stared at the cops, neither group saying anything.

"You guys heard me!" Yelled the one officer, "What are you gang bangers doing in Castle Point?" Again, no one in either group answered the police officer.

"All right, who's car is this?" The one officer asked.

"Mine," said Blackie.

The officer looked at Blackie and Vito then looked at the Puerto Rican gang. "Okay," he said, looking at Blackie, "take your car and

---

11 Faggots in Spanish

get out of here. You guys all know that Castle Point is off limits to you downtown thugs. Now scram, all of you! You too!" He said, pointing his night stick at the Alkies. "Move!!" Vito and Blackie got into the car and drove off while the Alkies reluctantly moved on down towards Washington Street.

"That was a close one," said Blackie to Vito, as he drove down Hudson Street.

"Yeah," Vito said, "I had my hand on my burner the whole time."

"Whaddaya think, those spics weren't packing too? Six against two!" Blackie shook his head, "Fugetaboutit, we're lucky those cops came around. They knew what was going down; saved our asses, that's for sure."

"Fucking Alkies, Jackson Street spics, that's all they are; just Jackson Street spics!"

"Yeah, we gotta tell Aldo what happened later on. Right now, we gotta call the girls, okay?"

"Yeah sure," said Vito, "that's a good idea. What time do you want to pick them up?"

"Say, eight o'clock. Then we can take them over to my place and see what happens, okay?"

"Sounds good to me," said Vito. "Just take me over to Saint Ann's, I gotta pick up my little brother. He's supposed to be playing basketball at the Rec Center with Father Joe today. I'll see you and the babes tonight, okay?"

"Cool!" said Blackie heading towards Saint Ann's Rec Center on Jefferson Street.

Blackie left Vito off in front of the center and sped off. Vito stood there until the car turned the corner. Then he walked to the candy store on the corner and called his date, Angela. She had a nice voice over the telephone. She said that eight o'clock was fine with her, and because he wanted to kill time, he talked to her two dimes worth. He hung up and strolled over to the center to pick up Dominic.

He had hardly spoken a word to Dominic in the morning. Because he had a hangover, he had yelled at him. Now, he was sorry and wanted to make it up to the kid.

Dominic wasn't a bad kid. Yeah, he was hanging out on the block shooting craps and who knows what else. But jeez, that is where they were living. What the hell was the poor kid supposed to do? I mean the kid had to have friends, right? He saw Dominic shooting hoops with some kids his age.

"Hey, douche-bag," he yelled at him, "waddaya doin'?

Dominic turned around and yelled back, "What does it look like I'm doing, jerk off?"

Vito laughed, the kid was definitely was street, even at ten years old. "Listen Dom, I'm gonna shoot some hoops myself," he said. "Tell me when you wanna go eat."

Vito took off his jacket and carefully put his pistol in one of the sleeves. Then he rolled up the sleeves of his shirt, took a basketball from one of the racks and went out on the court to shoot some hoops.

Standing at the foul line, he aimed and shot. The ball splashed through without touching the rim. Pleased with himself, he shot a second and third time, watching the ball drop through the hoop again. Now, dribbling the ball around the court he continued to make one basket after another. It had been over a year since he had played basketball and was proud that he had not lost his touch.

"That's pretty good shooting," a voice behind him said.

Vito turned around and saw Father Joe standing behind him smiling. "Thanks Father," he said continuing to sink another basket.

"Vitucch[12] what happened. I haven't seen you in the center for over a year, or in Church for that matter." Father Joe said, looking Vito in the eyes concerned.

"I've been busy, Father," said Vito.

"Too busy to come to church or even stop in to say hello? I see your mother in Mass every Sunday with your brother Dominic. It's not easy on her with your father away. Your presence and support would be comforting for her, to say the least."

Vito stopped dribbling the basket ball and smoothed his hair. "Just busy, Father, that's all, just busy."

"Really?" Father Joe said, "too busy for God and your family?"

"Maybe I'll start coming around again," Vito said.

"Sure, God would love that, your Mom would love it and so would I. Maybe you could get some of those Black Hawks you hang with to start coming to Mass again. You could be an example."

Vito looked at him suspiciously, "How do you know that I'm a Hawk, Father?"

Father Joe smiled putting his hand on Vito's shoulder, "Son, I was born and raised in this neighborhood. I was an 'Iron Duke' before God called me to be a priest. Don't you think I know what's going on in my own parish? Gang banging is something you can't keep a secret."

"You don't like the Hawks, do you Father?" Vito said, defensively.

Father Joe shrugged his shoulders. "Son, I don't think much of gangs in general. Where does it ultimately lead you? Crime, prison, worst case scenario, dead on the street. No, my boy, I don't think much of gangs at all. Thank God I was called out of that life years ago. Now, I try and help kids come out of that destruction."

"You were an 'Iron Duke,' Father?"

"Yes, I was."

"Well, whatever, Father, the Black Hawks are number one on the street. We get respect, we get girls, we have cash."

---

12 Vitucch, Sicilian slang for Vito.

Father Joe shook his head sadly, "You want me to walk away while you put on your jacket?" He asked.

Vito looked at him stepping back a little.

"You have a pistol in that jacket pocket, don't you? You're afraid I'm going to see it."

Vito stared at him. He didn't know what to say or do or how far he could trust Father Joe not to call the cops on him. Father Joe Altamara served as the parish priest in Saint Ann's Roman Catholic Church. He felt that he was trying to make a difference in the depressed neighborhood he had grown up in. Every juvenile he was able to bring to the center and back to church was someone he felt he had saved from a life of crime and ultimate destruction. It was a tough job to go out and drag boys off the street corners and make them want to change their lives around.

The neighborhoods of Hudson County New Jersey: Hoboken, Jersey City, Union City, Bayonne and Weehawken were infested with gangs. The Black Hawks, the Crazy Eights, the Alkies, the Latin Kings, the Washington Street Giants, The Polish Nation, the Irish Clovers, the Monroe Street Buddies, and Company K were just a few of the gangs that fought and terrorized the neighborhoods. They fought for the sheer joy of bloodying and mauling one another. No insult was so slight that it could not be used as an excuse for a violent episode or riotous rumble. Every day and night, Father Joe was faced with the insurmountable problems of his parish neighborhood. However, there was the belief that he was doing something worth while, and each boy that he saved from the gangs was a personal victory. Now, he watched Vito squirm as the kid looked at his jacket and wondered what to do with his gun.

"Go ahead, put on your jacket, I don't care either way," he said, disgusted.

Vito slipped his arm into the sleeve putting the pistol into his jacket pocket, where it bulged and sagged. "So, did you ever carry when you were an 'Iron Duke?" he asked, nervously.

"No, I was too smart to carry one of those things. All it can do is get you into more trouble than you can imagine."

"Aw, it's no big deal Father, everyone carries now. Ya gotta be packing nowadays or you don't know where you're living. I wouldn't ever really use it."

"Then why carry it? Why don't you give it to me and I'll get rid of it for you?" Said Father Joe, pleadingly.

"No way!" said Vito, shaking his head. "I paid big bucks for this and I'm keeping it. What the hell am I talking to you for anyway," he said, disrespectfully. "That's why I never come around, you're always trying to reform a guy! What the hell do I have to reform for? I don't do anything wrong!" He turned his back on Father Joe, walking off the court.

"If you're not doing anything wrong, what do you need a gun for?" Father called after him.

Vito stopped and turned toward him. "Listen Father, you're a good guy but maybe you better mind your own business!"

Father Joe walked towards him with his hand out. "Vito, you're a smart kid, you're not stupid. Why don't you just give me that gun before you get into something you can't get yourself out of?"

Vito backed away from him. "No, and you better not rat me out to the cops if you know what's good for you!"

"Why, are you gonna wack me, dump in the river? Is that who you really are?"

"Never you mind who I am, just leave me alone if you know what's good for you," snarled Vito. "I'm getting my little brother and gettin' outta here!" Then he turned and walked away. "Just remember what I said about ratting me out."

"I heard you," said Father Joe, sadly. "But any time you want to get rid of that piece just give it to me and I'll get rid of it for you. That's the best advice I can give you, son."

"Thanks for nothing, Father!"

"You're welcome, Vito. When will I see you again?"

"Never!"

"Come back whenever you like, the church is always open and Christ is always waiting for you. Or you can stop by the friary to talk and have a cup of coffee."

Without answering him, Vito went to pick up Dominic. He was silent, as they walked across Fourth Street up towards Washington Street and over to Shaffer's Diner. Father Joe had disturbed him. Maybe he was right about the gun. Hell, he never used it, and even the thought of using it on someone made him shudder. He didn't even like the thought of using a knife on a guy. He thought of Joey Pazzo slicing that spic's face the other night, the way his face opened up with the blood spitting out on the street. Well, he just didn't like it at all. But he couldn't let the other guys know that because he was a Black Hawk and he wasn't supposed to be afraid of anything.

Now, he had another worry. He had beat the shit out of Joey Pazzo, and Joey wasn't the kind of guy to let something like that pass. He wasn't the kind of guy to come right back at you. Joey would just save the revenge up for a long time, and then when you were least expecting it, zap!! The crazy bastard would knife you in the back or crack your skull from behind. But still, maybe Father Joe was right. He didn't need a gun, but you had to have one to be in the Black Hawks. He didn't know what to do. Father Joe had confused him. That's why he didn't like going to church and all that crap. He had enough on his mind without being preached at by some self-righteous priest.

"I want to stop in the apartment for a minute," He said to Dominic as they walked home. "You wait here for me."

"I gotta come upstairs and go to the bathroom."

"Okay, but hurry up, I have a date tonight."

"Fuck!" Dominic said, "You going out again?"

"Hey, watch the language," Vito said to his brother. "You're gonna slip and talk like that around Mom."

"She don't even know what it means. Now, if I said it in Italian, *fanculo*, then I'd get the belt," said Dom, laughing.

"Knock it off any way," Vito said, "it's not respectful."

"*Fanculo, fanculo, fanculo, vaffanculo anche a te!!*[13]" Dominic sang, dancing around the sidewalk.

"Damn," laughed Vito, "you are such a little asshole!"

"Can't you break your date?" Dom looked at him pleadingly. "Momma's working late again and I told you that I get scared all alone. That moron, Joey Pazzo, keeps staring at me. I thought you said he wouldn't bother me any more."

"Staring at you, ain't bothering you!" Vito said, exasperated.

"But I don't like the way he looks at me."

"Listen, Dom, they're his eyes and he can look whereever he wants to. Don't make more of it than it is. Jeez, you such a pain in the ass."

"I don't want to be by myself!" Dominic looked as though he was going to cry.

"Tomorrow night, I'll hang with you okay? Now stop being such a baby."

"Is the girl you're going out with hot?" Are you gonna get laid? Is she a piece of ass?" Dom said, pumping his fist.

---

13 Fuck, Fuck, Fuck and Fuck you too!!

Vito threw his eyes in the air shaking his head, "ten years old" he said to himself, and walked up the three flights of stairs to their apartment with Dominic in tow. He opened the door with his key.

"Okay, Dom, now go to the bathroom and do what you gotta do," he said, walking into the bedroom.

While his brother was in the bathroom, Vito changed into a high collared shirt. Opening his dresser draw, he took out a shoulder holster that he had recently purchased. He tucked his pistol in the holster and put on his sports jacket. The gun felt good and snug strapped under his left arm. He looked in the mirror, turned up his collar and combed his hair back with a little 'Brylcreem.' He felt sharp and ready for action, like a real Mafioso. That was the ultimate plan after all, to be a made guy in the Messina family. Numbers and slot machines and the black market paid off; not working like hell in a factory or in Todd's ShipYard, where the foreman was always up your ass. Where they could fire you whenever they felt like it; or getting thrown in jail for taking numbers on the job like his father did. His Dad was just trying to make a little extra for his family. Who was he really hurting anyway? Now, look what his poor mother and brother were going through with his father in the can and all. Fuck that shit, man, being a made guy with the Messina family was the real deal. Then, he would have the cash to help his family, have a sharp ride like Aldo Pinto had and have a hot babe like Joey Messina had on his arm. That was the plan, man, that was it in a nut shell. What the hell did Father Joe know anyway?

Chapter 5

The girls were waiting for them on the corner as they coasted the car to the curb, and Vito was excited to see Angela again. She was as pretty as he remembered her to be the day before. When she got into the car, she slid next to him putting her head on his shoulder. Her fingers felt slim and cool; she smelled wonderful and he felt protective and strong as he held her hand and pressed it gently. The car breezed along Route 3 as they left the city and drove into the suburbs. Vito tilted Angela's head back and kissed her, a long lingering kiss to which she responded as his hand slipped into her blouse.

"I really like you," he said.

"I like you too," she whispered to him. She stroked his hair kissing him again.

The cool night air flowed around them as the convertible sped along; the music from the radio was smooth and dreamy as the Happenings sang, 'See you in September.' Again, he kissed her and this time he felt her body relax as he pulled her closer, his libido surging as her tongue found his. He spun into space as the wild, passionate tumult of youth, heat and blood raced through their bodies. The breeze delighted them as they sped along the highway on this hot summer night.

"I'm really getting turned on," Angela said, smiling up at Vito.

"Me too," he said, taking her hand and putting it on his hardness.

She kept her hand on him, "Do you really like me?" she asked, moving her hand up and down.

"I think I'm in love," he said, laughing.

Just then, Blackie stepped on the brakes stopping the car. "Hey V, why don't you drive a little while I get in the back with my girl? I'd like to get some lovin' too. What am I the friggin' chauffer?"

"Great timing, Blackie, really great!" Vito moaned. "Come on," he said to Angela, "let's get up front, I'll drive awhile."

Angela pouted her lips, "We can play as you drive, I can still be a naughty girl," she said, looking down at his manhood.

"Get in the back!" Vito said to Blackie.
Blackie and his girl hopped into the back seat and started going at it right away; as Angela slid over and pressed herself against Vito's shoulder. Vito started up the car and they continued driving westward down Route 3.

Blackie and his date, Anna, were becoming more active in the back seat. It was obvious that he was actually getting laid. But not before she told him she didn't do that kind of stuff and who did he think he was trying that on her? What kind of girl did he think she was? But her protests were just a prelude to the inevitable, so she didn't feel like such a pushover.

"You don't think I'm going that far, do you?" Angela whispered, nervously. "I want you to know that I do not do that on a first date."

"Don't worry, sweetie," said Vito. "I really like you. You don't have to do anything you don't want to do."

She smiled and kissed his neck as he drove the car back up the highway to Hoboken. "We can still do this," she said, moving her hand up his leg.

"Yes, we can!" he said, catching his breath.

Back at Blackie's apartment, Blackie and Anna were in his bedroom with the door locked. Vito was sitting on the couch with Angela in his arms. The lights were low and the Moody Blues were playing on the radio. Angela lay looking up at him, her breathing soft and relaxed. There was no need to speak or to say anything, for they both understood how they felt. There would be no telling the guys how he made out with her; no graphic exaggerated sexual details that would make her look cheap. Some of the guys like Joey, Anthony, and even Blackie couldn't understand how he felt, but it was none of their business. To him, they were idiots, with their jeering, filthy language and tall tales about the girls they were with. Their mocking of anything that didn't conform to their brutal, vicious, mean gang world. Now that he found something clean, soft and beautiful with Angela, everything would be different. Tomorrow he would give his gun to Father Joe, quit the Black Hawks and start going to school regularly. As he looked into Angela's eyes, it all made sense now. The straight life, the good life, with a sweet lovely girl by his side, it all made sense. If he went to school, graduated and maybe went to college, he wouldn't have to work in a factory or the shipyard. He could be something, else something better. All of this realization came just because of a beautiful girl.

Angela moved gently and kissed him. "What are you thinking about?"

"You, us, together."

"I'm glad," she sighed. "I really like you, Vito. You're who I was waiting for."

Vito's heart almost exploded. "I don't want you going with any other guys," he said.

"I won't, I'm your girl from now on." They kissed and kissed and kissed as time just flowed and the music played.

In the next room, they could hear Blackie and Anna going at it with the headboard banging against the wall. Vito smiled at Angela and said,"I guess they're really going at it."

"Your friend doesn't waste any time," she agreed. "But understand, that I'm not like Anna." she said, shaking her head.

"I know you're not," he said, "I'm in no hurry. I feel different about you, I want you to know that you're special to me, understand?"

She stroked his hair while kissing him. "Yes, now let me just lie here in your arms; it's nice."

Later that evening, Vito drove the car as they took the girls home. Blackie continued groping Anna in the back seat, as he tried to get one last score in before the night was over.

Both girls lived in the same four family walk up on Fifth and Park Avenue. It was a nicer neighborhood than the boys came from. The streets and sidewalks were noticeably cleaner.

"Here we are," said Vito, as he pulled the car up in front of the girls apartment house. As Anna got out of the car, she smoothed down her skirt while waiting for Blackie to get out of the car and walk her up to her apartment. Her dress and blouse were completely wrinkled, her hair was a total mess and her lipstick was smeared all over her face. Angela got out with her. Vito took Angela's hand and walked her up to her parents apartment. They kissed goodnight with promises of tomorrow. She ran lightly up the steps, turned, waved goodbye and was gone.

Blackie was still all over Anna as she tried to push him off of her. "My parents are home, you pig!" She said angrily. "Now, get off of me! Jeez, what more do you want?"

Vito pulled Blackie away from her leading him to the car. "Come on man, let her alone now! It's time to go home!"

"Did you get laid?" Blackie asked Vito. "I did! Man oh man, did I ever give it to her! Did you bang Angela?! Yes or no, tell me man, did you?!"

"None of your fucking business!" said Vito indignantly, looking at Blackie like he was a piece of dirt. "And, don't ask me that again! You're an idiot!"

"What's up your ass?" Blackie said, offended. "I just wanted to know, that's all."

"And, I'm just telling you to mind your own business, that's all, okay?"

"Okay, okay, ya don't have to get all tough about it. I mean like we're friends and all. Friends tell each other that kind of shit."

"Yeah, yeah, just shut up," Vito said, shaking his head in disgust. Yes, tomorrow everything was going to change, everything.

Chapter 6

Mr. Cohen looked sternly at Vito and Blackie, as they swaggered into the classroom fifteen minutes late. He found it difficult to control the anger he felt as he watched the boys arrogantly dismiss his authority; as they pushed past him and sat in their respective seats. Young smirking wiseguys, they needed a good swift kick in the ass. That's what they sorely needed and richly deserved, he thought to himself.

Mr. Cohen slammed his hand down on the desk, demanding the class to quiet down. He looked at these two delinquents who just disrupted his classroom. The hostile faces of Blackie and Vito stared back at him. Despite himself and all of his liberal progressive training, he hated them.

"You two," he pointed at Vito and Blackie, "come up here."

"Who, us?" Vito said, turning and looking at Blackie. "Is this fucking Jew talking to us?" He said, shaking his head in mock disbelief. The room exploded with laughter as Mr. Cohen heroically held back his rage at these disrespectful lowlife hooligans who not only showed contempt for him but for an entire education system which he had given his entire life to advance and promote.

"Mr. Vito Fierro and Mr. Giacomo Corello, come up to the front of the classroom immediately or I will call the Director of Discipline and have you thrown out of this class and the school!"

Vito turned to Blackie laughing, "Giacomo? Blackie, the Jew called you Giacomo. Is that your name?"

"No," said Blackie. "It's jockstrap! Mr. Cohen, just call me Jockstrap Corello. And I'll call you a yellow, mealy-mouthed, pussyfied Kike. Too bad Hitler didn't shove you in the ovens with the rest of you cowardly pricks."

At that, Mr. Cohen flew across the room swinging a thirty six inch yardstick at Blackie's head. "You stupid, contemptuous, profane piece of human garbage!!" He swore in a bitter rage, continuing to swing the yardstick at Blackie.

Blackie ducked, running backwards while laughing and taunting Mr. Cohen. The class was now in total disarray. However, Mr. Cohen was not to be dissuaded as he continued his frenzied assault on this blasphemous delinquent. Blackie backed up against the cloak room doors trying to avoid the swinging yardstick. At that point, Vito jumped in grabbing Mr. Cohen from behind pinning his arms. The teacher spun around sending Vito flying across the classroom.

"Hey teach," one of the students yelled at him, "you're a real Hercules."

He smashed the ruler down across the student's desk. The force of the blow snapped the wood in two. The class rocked with more laughter as his face flushed. Mr. Cohen leaned against the blackboard, his head bowed in defeat and impotence.

Just then, Vito raised himself off the floor as he and Blackie rushed in, pinning the teacher against the wall. "You touch us again, teach, and we'll beat your Jew brains out! Understand?"

He pushed the two boys away with one powerful shove, for he was a big man. "Now, sit down and be quiet!!" he bellowed. But it was no use. All of his authority was gone. How the hell could he teach a class when these little bastards made his life so miserable? Why wasn't he allowed to just haul off and beat the shit out of this Blackie? Why couldn't he just smack the shit out of this Vito prick. When he was a kid, who would ever even think of talking back to a teacher? But now, he had to use all the damn instructional tools and psychological approaches that were successful only in these new liberal textbooks. They weren't useful in a real classroom full of punks that didn't give a damn about learning or what he was trying to teach them. If only he could keep his temper, but obviously it was no longer possible. He spent more time breaking up fights and trying to quiet an unruly student body than he ever did teaching.

"Fuck this shit, I'm done," said Blackie. "Come on, Vito, let's blow this joint! We're outta here, man!"

"Go, get out of here, leave! Go on, get the hell outta my class room and don't come back!"

Blackie looked at Mr. Cohen in mock surprise. "Don't you like me, teach? Hey guys," He said turning to the class, "The teach don't like me! Now come on, is that nice?"

"No!! That's messed up!" They answered in unison. The class stomped and yelled and paid no attention to Mr. Cohen's orders to be quiet. As they knew intuitively that he had lost control of the class, the bedlam and uproar became more wild and violent, more rowdy and gross. He looked at all of them with a perfect hatred. He left the classroom slamming the door behind him. Storming up to the principal's office in a rage, he yelled, "Mr. Matthews, take this as my immediate resignation!"

Mr. Matthews wheeled back in his chair, "What's the problem?!" He asked from behind his desk, "Is there a problem?!"

"Problem?!" Cohen acted as if he were ready to fall headlong into insanity. "A problem is an understatement! I've got a classroom full of congenital hoodlums and they are completely out of control!" He gritted his teeth and his hands were trembling. "I was physically assaulted, thrown against the wall and called a string of antisemitic slurs from a bunch of antisocial, lowlife cretins that the state calls underprivileged youth. And don't you dare tell me that I'm not a good disciplinarian; that somehow it's my fault. Every teacher in this school is in the same boat with these inbred third world monsters. The Italians, Puerto Ricans, Polocks, Irish trash, just let me take a good swing at all of them and you'll see discipline!"

"You know I can't allow that."

"I know and that's why I'm outta here! Fuck this school, fuck them and fuck you and your liberal, pansy, paddy cake policies that allow this kind of shit to go on. I quit!! You will get my resignation in the mail! I never want to see this school or this town again, good bye!" He walked out of the principal's office and he never returned.

Mr. Matthews walked down the hallway towards the classroom where all the noise was coming from. He was furious. And no, this was not the first time a teacher had resigned over these unruly adolescents. Boy oh boy, did he wish it was the good old days when a teacher could take a rod to a rebellious teenager's back. That's what was needed now. Not this new 1960's Dr. Spock bullshit that the Board of Education was now spewing. He walked into the riotous room, stood there for a moment with his hands on his hips, then pointed at the entire class.

"All of you," he bellowed, "are suspended from school until you bring at least one of your parents! And, if you don't have them here in at least two days, I will permanently expel each and every one of you. Then, the state will send you to a special school for delinquent behavior. Believe me, you will not enjoy the change! Furthermore, any of you found loitering in the halls or on school grounds will be immediately turned over to the police."

Well, that was that. Vito and Blackie walked out of the school not really caring if they were suspended, or expelled. Whatever Principal Matthews had said meant little or nothing to them. They decided to go over to the club to hang out for awhile and then give the girls a call about going out later that night. Vito still had hundreds of dollars in fugazi tens and twenties so they were living large at this moment in time.

Vito forgot all about his promise to himself to quit the Hawks and try to go legit. Hell, he wasn't made for that legit crap. As long as he had enough dough to hang out and take out his new girlfriend Angela he was fine and life was good. He decided not to even tell his mother that he was suspended. The poor woman had enough on her plate without having to worry about this suspension shit. Besides she could hardly speak English let alone have to listen to some American teacher read her the riot act concerning her son. No, Vito decided to ere on the side of silence.

They walked into the Black Hawks club room where Aldo, Anthony, and this Neapolitan kid Alberto were cutting up four pounds of marijuana for distribution on the street.

"Hey guys," Aldo said looking up from his work slipping weed into small nickle bags. "Just in time to help cut up this pot."

"Yeah sure, no problem." Blackie said. "Hey you guys wanna laugh? We just got kicked outta school. Like for good, ya know, like for good, like we ain't never going back!"

"Good," said Aldo, "now you can help move this shit on the street. Everybody take twenty nickle bags and hit Central Ave. in Jersey City. With all those hippies and niggers hanging out you shouldn't have any trouble getting rid of all of it."

"What's our cut of this shit?" Asked Alberto.

"Sixty/Forty like everything else. You guys get to keep sixty percent of the profit and the club gets the forty percent."

"So on twenty nickle bags that's one hundred dollars total and on a sixty/forty split we get to keep sixty bucks!" Said Anthony.

"Yeah, you got it Einstein." Said Aldo laughing, "Boy I got a crew of friggin geniuses here."

Blackie elbowed Vito, "See when your a Hawk ya never have to go scrounging for a job. Look at this shit, one, two, three and were already pulling in sixty bucks a day."

Vito reflected on what Blackie just said. His poor mother breaking her ass in a sweat shop for $1.60 and hour, wasn't making that much. And those double time shifts were killing the poor woman, and she couldn't even be home with Dominic and watch the kid grow up.

"Hey Vito, Anthony said, I saw your little brother before and he looked all beat up, he was walking up Monroe St. crying."

"What?" Vito said concerned. "You sure it was my brother?"

"Yeah, little Dominic, right? Sure I know who your brother is. The kid looked all smacked around and was balling. I don't know what happened, but just thought I should tell ya."

"Thanks!" said Vito leaving the club and running out of the door. "What the fuck did this little asshole get himself involved in now" he said to himself as he ran down Adams and turned down fourth onto Monroe. From the corner he saw Dominic walking up the tenement stairs. He ran up to him and as Dominic looked at him, he saw that the kid's face was red and he was crying.

"What happened?" he asked Dom.

Dominic grabbed Vito around the waist, buried his head in his brothers chest and started crying.

"What? What happened? Vito said rubbing his brother's head. He looked closely at Dominic's face. There were slap marks and bruises starting to turn purple on his cheeks and forehead. Vito got down on his knees took Dom's face in his hands. "What happened, tell me, who the hell did this to you?"

Dominic dropped his head and started balling again. "I can't, I can't tell you." he said shaking his head as he wept.

"Well your gonna tell me, damn it!" demanded Vito. "And your gonna tell me right now! Now spit it out!!"

First Dominic whispered then he became enraged, screaming and punching Vito in the chest. "It was that mothafucka Joey Pazzo. It was Joey Pazzo! He pulled me into that ally next to Romano's and started to smack me, for no reason!" Dominic started to scream and cry at the same time. "That fuck, that dirty fuck, took out his dick and wanted me to jerk him off, then he pulled my head down and he, he," Dominic started to sob again.

"He what? What did he do?" Vito demanded horrified.

"He wanted me to put his dick in my mouth!!" Dominic screamed, "He wanted me to do it, but I didn't, I twisted away from him and tried to run away but he grabbed me by the hair and started smacking me in the face. I grabbed his hand and bit his finger, I tried to bite it off V, I tried to bite his fucking finger off." Dominic started to cry again, "He yelled and I kept trying to bite his finger off, I really tried, *figlio de putan bastardo,* I tried to bite it off as hard as I could. Finally he punched me in the head, I fell down and I ran away. Vito why would someone want to put their penis in your mouth? Why? Why?" He started to cry and punch Vito in the chest again.

Vito was beside himself with rage, and guilt for leaving his little brother alone so much of the time. But this, this was beyond outrageous.

"That son of a bitch Joey is a sick fuck, come with me Dom, were gonna ruin this low life mutt, right now, today!" He took Dominic by the hand and ran up the stairs of the next door tenement house.

Dragging his brother along he scaled the three flights of stairs and began pounding on Joey's apartment door. Joey opened the door as Vito bulldozed his way into the apartment, seizing Joey by his huge ears and smashing him into the dining room table, the boys grappled as they tore and punched at each other in a furious life or death struggle. Joey broke away from Vito's grasp backing against the wall he picked up a ceramic statue of Saint Joseph that was altered on the table.

"Okay, you asked for it," growled Joey using the statue as a club. He rushed Vito attempting to smash his skull with it. Vito backed up and pulled out his revolver but Joey swung the heavy icon catching Vito on the side of the head with it. Vito fell backwards dropping his gun onto the oriental carpet. Quickly, Joey swung again hitting Vito with a vicious strike to his shoulder. Vito fell to the floor, raising his arms blocking and covering himself as Joey tried to smash his head with the heavy icon.

Dominic seeing that his brother was in serious trouble, picked the pistol off the carpet hitting Joey in the back of the head with the butt of the gun. The sudden pain made Joey drop the statue as he raised his hands to his head Vito hit him squarely in the throat. Spittle bubbled at the corners of Joey's mouth as he momentarily gasped for breath, then blindly dove at both brothers. There was only one thing he wanted to do now, and that was to kill. He grabbed hold of Vito's throat as Dominic jumped on his back frantically striking him on the head with the gun butt. With one violent shrug of his shoulders Joey hurled Dominic off his back onto the floor. He now held Vito down determined to choke the life out of him. Vito struggled wildly gasping for air under Joey's powerful strangle hold on his throat, his eyes bugging out and rolling backwards.

Dominic got up from the floor stumbling towards Joey, put the barrel of the gun to Joey's head and instinctively pulled the trigger.

There was a sharp muffled crack, as the 22.cal bullet entered Joey's brain, he wavered, looked at them for a moment, fell sideways as blood and water poured out of his head, collapsed and died.

Dominic wiped his flushed face and stared with wonder at the gun. Vito pushed Joey off of him and got to his knees looking at Dom and then at Joey. For the first time realizing that the toy that he so bravely carried around was in reality a deadly weapon. The room was silent except for their heavy breathing. The silence screamed about them in the vortex of sudden death and murder.

Vito gulped and slapped Dominic in the face. "What the hell did you do that for?"

Dominic the little ten year old boy shook his head dumbly and continued to stare at the gun and the body. Blood soaking from the head wound discoloring the oriental carpet as the stain grew larger and bright red.

Vito slapped Dominic again. "You stupid fuck, you killed him!"

Dominic started to cry, "He was killing you, he was choking you, you were turning blue! If he killed you I'd be all alone!" He started sobbing helplessly.

Vito took Dominic by the shoulder and pushed him towards the door then stopped. Silently he opened the door and peered into the corridor. It was empty, He pushed Dominic ahead of him, shut the door and tiptoed to the stairs. Luck was with them, it was early in the day and everyone in the tenement was out working. With sweat running down their faces they forced themselves to descend slowly and quietly. Then walking to the front door Vito peeked out looking down either side of Monroe, the street was empty as the bright summer sun hit them full in the face. In ten steps they were on the sidewalk walking nonchalantly towards home. Vito was sure that no one had seen them leave. But what about their entry into Joey's tenement house, had anyone seen them rush in? He didn't know and that scared him.

Stumbling along in a stupefied daze, Dominic was still holding the gun as they walked down the street. Vito looked at him and gasped. "Holy shit, gimmie that thing!" he pulled the piece out of his brother's hand and stuck it in his pants pocket. Then he dragged the kid up the stairs of his building and shoved him into the apartment.

Vito dropped to his knees took Dom's by the shoulders and looked him in the eyes. "Listen up Dom, ya gotta snap outta this. You can't tell anybody, no one about this. This shit is murder, we can't even claim self-defense because we were in his apartment! Shit, we can never say a fucking thing about this not even to mom or dad when he gets home. *Capisci*, understand? Tell me that you understand!"

Dom nodded still staring right through Vito intense gaze. "Yes I understand."

"Say it in Sicilian, it means more, say it in Sicilian!"

Dominic looked into his brother's eyes *"Si capisco cosa stai dicendo."*

The deep intensity and profundity of the kids statement reassured Vito that Dominic's lips were sealed. "Okay, now I have to get rid of this gun." Vito said aloud. He went to the sink and soaked the pistol in soap and water then wiped it off and wrapped it in a dishtowel. He had to take this thing and dump in the river. He would go down to the First Street peer at night and throw cursed thing into the Hudson.

Just as he was planning his next move there came a screaming a howling from across the ally way. Vito and Dominic ran to the bedroom window looking out over the fire escape into the next door tenement. What they saw gripped their hearts as sorrow, fear and bile came up their throats. Mrs. Pazzolino, Joey's mother, had just come home from work and found her son. Through the ally way window they could see her spinning around in circles, cries of agony and despair she was pulling her hair and wailing for God to help her. The shrill screeching and lamenting went on and on until the boys heard police sirens screaming up Monroe Street.

Vito pulled Dominic by the arm. "Come on Dom, we gotta go down stairs, the whole neighborhood is in the street trying to see what happened. If we don't go down it'll look suspicious. Come on we gotta go down stairs and hang on the sidewalk like were curious." He pulled the still uncomprehending Dominic along with him as they descended the tenement and walked out onto the crowded sidewalk. "Remember he whispered into Dom's ear, you don't know nothin, code of the street Dom, code of the street, *Omerta*[14], right?"

Dominic nodded his head "*Omerta*, code of the street;" he said. "*Non so niente, non ho visto niente, non dico niente*, I know nothing, I saw nothing, I say nothing."

They stood around the mulling crowd looking as curious as the rest of the neighborhood. People chatted and surmised the cause of Joey's murder. Everyone nodded knowingly saying that they all knew that the crazy bastard would meet his end one day. Yes they all had guessed the outcome of Joey's life years ago. Except for Joey's mother who even though she saw the inevitable, hoped against hope and prayed to God for a miraculous transformation of the son she loved so dearly.

The police questioned everyone as was standard operating procedure and as was standard on the street, no one heard or saw anything. Life on Monroe street went on as usual.

---

14 Omerta. The Sicilian code of Science, to never betray anything to the police.

Chapter 7

Back in their apartment, the boys sat at the dining room table, eating a pepper and egg frittata[15] which their mother had left them to eat. Dominic looked at Vito concerned.

"Maybe we better run away, get out of here before they come and take us away like they took Papa away."

"Just wait," said Vito, choosing his words carefully. "We have to be careful about running away. I'm pretty sure no one saw us leave Joey's place, and if no one saw us go in, then we're pretty safe."

"Really?" said Dominic nervously. "Would they put me in jail, like they did Papa?'

"Vito saw his little brother become tense and nervous. "Don't worry Dom, we're not gonna run anywhere. We'll just hang around and act like nothing happened and we don't know nothing! Right Dom, we don't know nothing?"

Dominic nodded his head. "We don't know nothing."

"Good boy! Just remember '*Omerta, the code of silence, is worth more than all the gold in Sicily.*' That's what Papa always says. So Remember, *Omerta.*"

Dominic touched his face, "my face is a little marked up."

---

15 Frtitata: Italian omlet.

Vito leaned over and touched his brother's face. "It's nothing. No one will be able to see it by morning. And I think I look alright except for this cut on my head where Joey hit me with that statue. It'll be alright, Dom. I'll call my girlfriend Angela and ask her to bring her friend Anna and I'll call Blackie, and we'll double date. You stay here and watch T.V. then go to bed. When Momma comes home be sure you don't start to cry and tell her what happened."

"I'm not gonna cry," Dom said. "I'm gonna be street, I'm not saying nuttin. I just wacked somebody, I'm gangster now!'

"Listen up, you little shit! You're not gangster, and you didn't kill anybody! Understand? You're ten years old, you're a kid and you didn't do anything, nothing wrong, nothing, do you hear, nothing!" Vito started to cry as he hugged Dominic close to him.

Dom hugged him back as the two brothers stayed locked in a fraternal embrace of love, concern, and fear. What tomorrow would bring, the boys did not know. The image of Joey lying dead on the oriental carpet with his eyes open and his head oozing blood. This binding secret that they shared was now almost too burdensome to bear and haunted their young minds.

"Remember," Vito said to his brother, "You tell no one, no one!" His voice was an iron gate that shut around the ten year old's heart.

The next morning Vito ran out of the apartment to the corner candy store to pick up a newspaper. Willy Quack, the owner of 'Turks Palace' the candy store clubroom, handed him the *Jersey Journal*. Vito threw a dime on the counter and quickly left the store.

"Where ya running to?" yelled Willy after him. "What's your hurry?

Vito walked down the street opening up the newspaper. *The Jersey Journal* had the headline splashed across the frontpage.

TEEN AGE BOY SHOT DEAD IN HIS APARTMENT
NO CLUES TO KILLER

Vito sighed a sigh of relief as he ran up the stairs of the tenement house. No clues to the killer, not killers. No clues. No nothing. They were in the clear. But they had to be careful.

Last night, he had gone out after dark and walked down to the First Street Pier, throwing the pistol into the Hudson River. He walked home praying to God that they would get away with this predicament. I mean, what was he supposed to do? That freak Joey Pazzo wanted his little brother to suck his dick. That sick disgusting bastard deserved what he got, a bullet in the head was too good for him. And little Dominic had just liberated himself from that loathsome act by killing Joey himself. You had to hand it to the kid, he had the balls to pull the trigger. So God had to bless them and let all this pass. In His justice, God had to exonerate them both.

However, all that was over now, the cops had no clues. "Thank you, God!" Vito cried, looking up to heaven. "Thank you Blessed Virgin Mary"! He felt like dancing the relief was so great. Dominic came out of the bedroom.

"What's up V?" he asked.

"I just got the morning paper and they said that they don't know who shot Joey. They have no clues. Man oh man, what a relief!"

"Yeah," said Dominic, "is there anything to eat?"

"Eat?" Vito looked stunned. "You're worried about food?"

"Yeah, I'm hungry, are you gonna make me breakfast?"

Vito looked at Dominic incredulously. "The kids hungry, he's hungry. We just got away with murder and the kid wants breakfast." He walked over to his little brother and rubbed his head. "You got the makings of a hit man kid." he said laughing.

"Yeah well just stop talking and make me breakfast before I put one in your head." Dom said seriously.

Vito stopped dead in his tracks, and looked at his brother. "Dom, this is no joke, you killed someone, do you understand that?"

"Yeah, I do, and he deserved it! I would do it again, that piece of shit wanted to put his penis in my mouth. I should have shot the son of a bitch twice. Maybe I should go over there and shoot his mother for having such a scumbag for a son. Yeah, I should shoot her in her fucking head and watch the blood spit out on the floor!" he said curling his lips sadistically.

Vito saw a drastic change in his brother, and it scared and distressed him. The kid didn't look the same. He wasn't acting the same. There seemed to be a disturbing coldness rising in his young heart. And Vito did not know how to suffer it. So he just ignored the child's callous ranting and started breakfast.

Vito hummed a song *"I'm a lucky fella and I've just got to tell her that I love her endlessly"* by Edison Lighthouse Band, as he dialed Angela's number from the candy store's phone booth. *"Because love grows where my Rosemary goes and nobody knows like me!"* The cops had no clues, boy was he relieved.

He was glad when Angela answered the phone and he smiled at the mouthpiece of the telephone as if she could see him. "You know," he said, and he marveled that he spoke with such calmness, "when your mother and father are never home it isn't easy to take care of things and I have a kid brother that I have to look after. So honest babe I'm sorry that I didn't call you sooner. But we can meet tonight, if that's okay with you?....Fine, that's great! And can you get Anna to come for Blackie? ... That's cool baby girl, 'cause Blackie likes her. Yeah I know, well, I'll tell Blackie to cool it with the getting laid stuff. But to tell you the truth, she shouldn't have put out so fast. Ya know when a chick does that a guy feels he can get it all the time, ya know?… So okay, everything is cool then, we'll pick you kids up at the same place, say about eight, okay?.. Good, fine, I'll be seeing you then, I can't wait, you're so hot. Yeah I know, thanks, see you then sweetie."

Vito picked up another newspaper from the counter of 'Turks Palace", and started reading the murder story as he stood there.

"Hey, didn't you just buy a newspaper?" Asked Willy the store owner.

"Yeah, but I left the paper home, I'm just reading about this murder of Joey."

Willy shook his head, "well I can't say that I'm surprised, that Joey was a frigging madman. It was only a matter of time before someone put one in his coconut. The fuckin kid would come in here and take a bottle of Coke and a pack of Twinkies and just walk out without paying. Like he was a cop on the beat or a mob guy or some kind of a guy with pull. Fuckin kid could pull this!" Willy said grabbing his crotch. "It was only a matter of time before someone ended him, ya know?"

"Yeah, Joey was a sick fuck," said Vito, as he read the story. The paper didn't carry many details except that Joey was bruised, as if he had been in a fight, and that he had been killed with a .22 caliber bullet that had punctured his brain. There were no clues, and no one had seen anyone suspicious entering or leaving the building. And as he read he hummed more brightly, *love grows where my Rosemary goes and nobody knows like me!"* That song had been playing in his head all day since he heard it on the radio this morning, with Cousin Brucie WABC the station that all New York and North Jersey listened to. He left the candy store throwing the newspaper back on the counter whistling brightly as he walked down Monroe Street.

He clapped his hands and waved them at Blackie as he opened the clubroom door. "Everything's fixed for tonight we got a date with the girls at eight tonight."

"Good, good, good," smiled Blackie, "I'm horney as hell."

"Listen up, you hornball," Vito said, slapping Blackie on the shoulder, "try and keep your hands off Anna, will ya, she's a little pissed that you were all over her like stink on shit the other night."

"Why? She put out like a friggin Coke machine, I didn't hear any complaints."

"Yeah, well Angela said that she don't want you to think that she's that easy, she felt like a whore, ya know."

"Fuck, I didn't rape her! She put out willingly, I don't remember her complaining!" Blackie said angrily.

"Okay, I know, but just try and been a gentleman tonight, okay? We got a good thing going with these girls and I don't want you to fuck it up."

"Yeah, yeah, yeah, okay already." Blackie said discouraged. "Jeez, a guy can't do anything with these broads."

Vito laughed, "You did plenty, buddy, plenty. So just try to keep it in your pants tonight okay?"

Chapter 8

The Fierro's sat around the kitchen table, Dominic occasionally glancing at Vito. Vito ate slowly concentrating on his food attempting to ignore his mother's questioning gaze. It was a Sunday afternoon and his mother was home from work this day. She had prepared a Sunday meal for the boys of eggplant parmigiana and a dandelion salad. She could have been working overtime this Sunday but Dominic was sick with a fever and she felt guilty about always leaving the boys alone.

"Something is not right in dis'a house!" She said shaking her fork at the boys. "Whadda happen here? Some thinga no a good in disa house! I know dis, you no lie to mamma, I know some thinga a no good! You tella me now!" She demanded, slamming her hand on the table.

"Ma, nothing is wrong!" Said Vito, "I told you a hundred times already, nothing is wrong. Dom and I are just alone all the time and things aren't the same. When papa gets out of jail things will be okay again, okay? Now stop asking!"

"You no get disrespectful to me, I'm a you mamma, and I know things. Dominic, what is the matter. You no eat, you have fever, you look all schupato (pale), something no good in dis'a house!"

"Jesus Christ ma, nothing is wrong! Now stop this cross examination, what are you, a friggin cop?" Cried Vito, rising from his chair.

"Hey, you boy, no say Jesus in a disrespectful way! First you disrespect me, and now you say Jesus in a bad way! Something is no good in dis'a home, I know!"

Dominic just sat there looking at Vito. Vito got up from the table shaking his head. "I didn't do anything!" he yelled. Then he realized that he was trembling. He sat back down and toyed with the food on his plate. "Why can't you just leave me alone? I told you that there is nothing wrong. I can't help it if somebody killed the crazy kid next door. I can't help it if Dom is playing craps in an ally. I can't help it if Pop's in jail. I can't help it if we live in a lousy stinking slum and there's no money. What the hell do you want out of my life any way?" He was raging now at his mother and she and Dominic were just looking at him as he ranted on and on.

"Basta! (enough!)" his mother yelled slamming her hand on the table again. "if your father were here he knock you stupido head off. You yell like a dis to your mama? How about the days pay I loose because I want to make you a nice dinner? You buy gold bracelet and I gotta work like a dog and you no give'a me nothing! You bum! You gangster! Yes I know Mafia, since I little girl. I see you go mafia! Do I ask you to go to work? No! I want you go to school be somebody in America not so you can be a Mafioso!"

"Mamma." Dominic said almost crying. "Vito didn't do anything wrong. He was just trying to help me, because Joey...."

Vito grabbed Dom's leg under the table and squeezed it hard. Dom shut his mouth immediately.

"And how are you watching your little brother?" His mother raised her eyes to the ceiling and spoke to God. "Does he look after him like a good brother? No! Too busy being a mafiosio, with gold

74

jewelry and a gun! Yes I know about the gun! I see it in your dresser! *Vergognoso!!* (shameful)!"

Vito threw down his fork on the table and rushed into his bedroom. Tears hung in the corners of his eyes, as he flung himself across the bed. The old lady was too damn much for him.

"Don't think you can get away from me, you gangster, *cattivo ragazzo disgraziata!* She opened the bedroom door and leaned across the foot of the bed. "I should slap'a you face *disgraziato*![16]"

"Mamma, please let him alone!" begged Dominic, "let him finish his supper, please!"

"Who's stopping him from eating? Not me! Get up!" she said to Vito, "and finish your supper!"

"I'm not hungry any more." His voice was muffled in the pillow.

Dominic approached the bed and touched his arm. "Come eat Vito."

"I said I'm not hungry any more. She's harassing the shit outta me. I can't take it any more. What the hell did I do anyway?"

"Get up," his mother said, "and come to the table, *Mafiosio!* I said enough. You a stupid boy, but not a bad boy! Come eat, I made nice *parmagiana,* now you sit and eat, okay?" She hesitated and then went back into the kitchen. She looked at Dominic, "tell him to come back and eat before everything gets cold."

"Come on V." his brother shook him-- get up now."

Vito washed his face and returned to the table. That was another thing he hated about the apartment, the bathroom being off the kitchen. As he sat at the table, he wished he didn't have to eat. His mother thought he wasn't hungry because of her bawling him out, but he wondered if she knew what it was like to have watched his little brother kill somebody and then having to keep his mouth shut about it, and worrying about Dominic, if he could keep his mouth

---

16 Disgraziato.. Disgrace or wretched one.

shut. I mean he was only ten years old and the kid almost slipped a minute ago.

As he sat at the table trying to pull himself together, it seemed as if his mother's scolding and cursing came from a distance. Although she sat right next to him, her voice seemed to come through a fog and it no longer bothered him. The cops suspected nothing and would never find out who killed Joey. Not from him they wouldn't. But what about Dominic? The cops were starting to question everyone in the neighborhood, and he didn't know what Dominic might say. If only Dom weren't such a little kid, he could be intimidated by the cops or fooled into telling what happened. Just look at the way he almost told their mother. He started to think about how the one detective looked at them when they were questioning them in the street. Why hadn't they asked him why his head was bleeding or why Dominic was standing there staring like a zombie.

He had to have an alibi, yeah and alibi, he was at the center playing basketball with Dom that day. Yeah that's it. He was going to start going to the center and hanging out with Father Joe. He was going to stop smoking reefer and drinking and get a job a real job. Maybe at the pencil factory or at Ferguson Propeller or at Maxwell House or maybe even at the shipyard. And he was going to make sure that Dom was at the church center with Father Joe every day. They would never be caught, but the fear would not leave him, and that was why he could not eat.

"Mamma, I'm sorry I caused you all this worry, I'll try to be better, I swear to God."

"How can I believe you?" His mother wailed. "You stay out late, carry a gun, don't go to school and you're going to get into more and more trouble with those gangsters you have as friends. Look at what happened to your friend Joey next door! Somebody killed him. For what did they do it? He was doing bad things! People don't kill you for nothing! Nothing in the apartment was stolen, no robbery, just killing! Because he was a bad boy!"

"Ma, please, you don't know when to stop! I said I would try to do better! Now please stop!" Vito looked over a Dominic, "would you like to go to the movies after supper? I don't have to meet with my girlfriend until eight o'clock so well have plenty of time."

"Yeah, let's go to the movies," said Dominic. "That spy movie *'Our Man Flint'* is playing at the Paramont, I wanna see it."

"I'm tired," his mother said. "You can go to the movies, I gotta go to work tomorrow. I lost enough money for today, so enough of this *disturbo!*"

Vito approached his mother and forced himself to kiss her on the cheek. "I'm sorry mamma, believe me." She would never know how sorry, he really was.

She got up from the table and kissed him back. "You go to the movies with your brother, be good to him, you only got one brother and who knows how long I'm gonna be around. Im'a so tired all the time. When I go, I wanna know that you two will be okay."

"Oh, here we go again, with the dying act. You're gonna outlive everybody momma, 'cause your killing everybody else with aggravation."

"Oh, you!" she said slapping him on the head. "You go now, leave me in peace for a while. Go, go, go," she said pushing him away. "Take Dominic and get the heck outta here! My God, I'm never alone, just to think and pray and wonder who I am." She picked up a dishtowel and started wiping down the table as she bemoaned her fate to God.

Chapter 9

The movie let out at six p.m. and Vito walked Dominic to the front of their tenement house at 404 Monroe Street. It was early enough for him to get ready to see Angela, so he ran up the stairs and into the bathroom to shave and clean up. Their mother was cleaning the apartment and would soon be going to bed. Her shift would start early tomorrow morning and she wanted to straighten up the place as much as possible before her hours at work would start again. Dominic came in and immediately turned on the television watching the new Batman series.

Vito cleaned up, shaved and put on some Old Spice cologne threw on a black crew neck shirt and a sports jacket, charcoal slacks and black leather loafers, slicked back his hair and checked himself out in the mirror. Satisfied with what he saw, he ran out of the apartment without saying goodbye to either his mother or brother. He didn't need any more negativity. He couldn't wait to see Angela and he whistled to himself as he left Monroe Street turning left onto Fourth Street heading up towards Washington Ave.

He saw Angela sitting at a table as he passed through the door of Shafers Diner, and the true joy of seeing her made his sullen face young and eager. Before each date with her he wondered if she was as he remembered, and each meeting he was again taken with her beauty. She was young, lovely, and desirable, and his. Angela waved to him as she saw him enter the restaurant, and he smiled as he quickly noted the blue and white sundress which accented her figure and the way her dark wavy hair fell spilled over her bare shoulders. Angela wore high heel sandals, and sheer stockings which accented her lovely legs.

"You look as hot as a firecracker," Vito said, kissing her.

"I don't know about that. I've been sitting here awhile and no one's tried to pick me up." she said smiling.

"Come on, let's get out of here and go pick up Blackie and Anna"

"Do you want to get something to eat?" She said.

"Yeah, but not here. Blackie and Anna are going to meet us at Helmers, that German restaurant on 11th and Washington." Vito stood up and pulled her chair back from the table.

As he walked with her, Vito was proud of the stares and whistles Angela received from guys who sat at other tables. Her hips swayed slightly, a provocative promise of her grace and desirability.

"Vito," she said, "your friend is going to be a good boy tonight, isn't he? Because Anna doesn't want to be groped all night like the last time."

"Don't worry about Blackie. I can keep him under control if I have to." He took her hand and led her out onto the street. "Let's get a cab, no use walking all the way down to Eleventh Street."

"Ooh, a cab," Angela said impressed, "can we afford that?"

"Hey, who ya wit here, baby? I'm Vito, the man with the plan!" He grabbed her and kissed her on the lips. She smiled and kissed him back. While seated in the taxicab she put her arms around him and kissed him slowly and sensually. He felt himself grow in stature and manhood as he held her in his arms.

As they stepped out of the cab in front of Helmers, Vito noticed Aldo Pinto standing at the checkroom counter and behind him stood Blackie and Mikey Sabatelli.

"Glad you could make it," said Aldo, after acknowledging the introduction to Angela.

"Make what?" said Vito, "Why are you guys here?"

"Why, we can't be here without your permission?" Said Mikey. "Blackie told us you were coming with your date so we figured we'd all come out together. Got a problem with that?"

"No, I got no problem, just didn't expect to see you guys here that's all. No beef, so drop the attitude, okay?" Vito took Angela's hand and led her into the dining area.

Mikey looked over at Aldo and shook his head. "He's getting to be a real wise guy."

"I know," Aldo said, with ominous patience.

Angela greeted Anna at the table where she sat with Blackie. The girls traded compliments on their wardrobe and decided to go to the ladies room. When the girls left, Mikey walked over to the table leaning over Vito and said, "Listen, I didn't like the way you spoke to me. Watch your P's and Q's, or else, okay big shot?"

Vito rose from the table and grabbed Mikey by the lapels of his jacket and pulled him forward. "Or else what?" Vito said. " Listen, Mikey, I think you're a good guy even though you were a friend of that idiot, Joey Pazzo. But I'm telling you, if you ever threaten me again, you'll see what I'm made of! Understand!?"

"Get your hands off me, you bastard," Mikey said quietly. You want to start a fight in here? This is a classy joint, the bulls will be here in a heartbeat."

Vito released him and stepped back.

Mikey smoothed the lapels of his jacket and did not look at Vito as he spoke. "I'm not forgetting this, Vito. I'll take care of you some other time, you can count on it."

"Yeah, fuck you," Vito replied, and whirled around as he felt someone's hand on his shoulder. It was Angela standing there with

Anna. He smiled at her and they sat at the table. Vito was still seething as he looked over at Blackie with his arm around Anna. "Anything wrong?" Blackie asked.

"No, nothing wrong. I just don't like that Mikey prick, he thinks he's a tough guy, and he was friends with that psycho, Joey. Just forget it and let's have a good time with the girls, okay?"

"Okay by me," said Blackie, as he reached under the table to fondle Anna.

Dominic stood on the corner of Monroe street waiting for some of his friends. It was Saturday morning and they were going to play a stick ball game with some kids from Adams Street. He wondered if he looked the same. He heard it said on the street that once you killed your first guy your appearance changed. He looked in the glass window of the candy store and didn't see any change, except that maybe his eyes were colder. He was a hard guy now, he was only ten and he killed his first man. Shit, nobody in his third grade class had killed anyone, he was sure of that. He looked at himself again, he was almost a made guy. I mean, he made his bones, he killed. So who was better than him? Not even his brother Vito had iced someone. No, he was the guy on the street now. Shit, they all better respect who he was. But the problem was no one knew that he had wacked Joey Pazzo, how could he earn street credit if no one knew about it?

"I did it." Dom said to himself. No matter how Vito figures it, "I'm the one who shot that piece of shit Joey in the head, I'm the one who pulled the trigger. If Vito had been able to kick Joey's ass in the first place I wouldn't have had to shoot him." Joey was crazy and waschoking Vito to death. So what could he do, he thought, Joey might have killed Vito, and he had to get the son of a bitch off of his brother. So now Joey was dead and he felt like a mafiosi, but nobody knew about it. Real hard guys, when they worried about a guy squealing or ratting, knocked off the guy who might get them in trouble, or disrespected them. And Joey had surely disrespected him by pulling out his stupid dick. It was driving him nuts when he thought about the look on Joey's face when he wanted him to touch him. So he had to be a hard guy and kill Joey, the bastard, the son of a bitch bastard!

"Good! I'm glad I killed him!" Dominic said to himself as he looked in the glass window pane seeing if he had changed. But now he wanted to tell somebody, he needed to brag on how brave and strong he was.

He walked into the candy store. Aldo Pinto and Mikey Sabatelli were sitting at the counter. "Hey what's up kid?" said Aldo, "Where's your brother?"

"How should I know?" said Dom. "Listen Aldo, I think I should be a Black Hawk."

Aldo and Mikey looked incredulously at him and laughed, rubbing his head. "Wait until you wearing big boy pants kid." Aldo said kidding him.

Dominic angrily pulled away from him. "I got more balls than any of you guys."

"Really," laughed Mikey, "have your balls even dropped yet? Dig this crazy kid, only what, ten and he wants to be a Hawk. Your still on his mother's tit, go home kid."

Chapter 10

Vito, Aldo, Blackie, and the rest of the Black Hawks sat on the uncomfortable high back benches in the anteroom of the Hoboken Police Station. Vito looked around noticing a crack in the wall that ran from the baseboard to the ceiling. The crack went across the ceiling, but it was uncomfortable leaning back to see how far it went, so he shut his eyes and in his head he sang an old Italian song that his Grandfather used to sing to him. The song comforted him and made him feel less afraid. He prayed to God that his alibi would stick. He saw no holes in it. For two hours now the detectives had been questioning the boys from the gang.

The boys slouched on the benches. Some rested their heads on the backs pretending to be asleep and indifferent to the questioning, while others tried to read newspapers and magazines, smoked or conversed in whispered voices. They all hated cops, because hating cops was the tough thing to do. It wasn't a personal hatred, just a general hatred of any authority, Police, teacher, or parent. It was the tough guy thing to embrace. If they were walking along the street talking and a squad car passed they would spit, curse or flip them the finger.

Now they were waiting to be questioned and each one wanted to show the others what a gangster he really was, to tell the detectives that he wouldn't talk without his lawyer present, like the real mob guys did. Why even if the bulls knocked him around, he wanted to baffle them with his hardness. Somewhere among them was the killer, and by sitting in close proximity to him gave them a vicarious thrill. They wouldn't tell the cops anything, and by being un-co-operative, vague, and arrogant, they would be helping the killer, sharing in the crime and putting one over on the cops, who were no good, who were always raiding their club and arresting their members for stupid things like crap games and selling reefer.

The door opened and one of the boys walked out. They looked at him and were disappointed, for he had not been beaten.

"You," the policeman pointed to one of the boys at random, "come in!"

They watched as Anthony swaggered defiantly into the room. The door closed and they relaxed as they waited their turn.

Aldo nudged Vito. "How much longer before they call us do ya think?"

Vito shrugged, "I don't know, but I'm sick of this shit. Fucking cops think they're big ya know? Psst, they ain't shit." he huffed.

"What do'ya think they'll ask us."

"I don't know!" said Vito shifting on the bench. "Friggin bulls can kiss my guinea ass."

The door opened again and the policeman ordered Vito, Aldo and Blackie to come in together. There was an electrical stirring among the other gang members and a quickened interest, because up until now each boy had been interrogated individually, and taking the three of them together meant something.

"Sit down boys," Detective Gilligan motioned to the chairs. He held out a pack of cigarettes. "Smoke?" he asked.

"No thanks!" The three said in unison.

"Now let me see," Gilligan said. "Which one of you is Aldo Pinto?"

"I am!" said Aldo.

"Then you're, Vito Fierro?"

"That's right."

"And you are Phillipo Carrozza also known as Blackie?"

"Yeah, what about it?" sneered Blackie.

"My name is Brian Gilligan. And I want you boys to know that I'm a friend of yours. I know you don't believe that," he laughed shortly, "and I guess you guys don't like cops. But we aren't bad guys, and when you get to know me you'll see that I'm regular. "Now," Gilligan loosened his tie. "I'll have to ask you some questions, and Miss Kramer here," he flicked his thumb towards the stenographer, "is gonna take down our conversation."

"Go ahead, shoot!" said Aldo leaning back in his chair and crossing his legs nonchalantly.

"Do you know who killed Joey Pazzolino?"

"No!" Aldo replied.

"And you?" Gilligan turned to Vito.

Vito could feel his voice tremble. "No."

"How about you?" The detective said, looking at Blackie.

"I don't know shit!" Said Blackie, leering at the cop.

"Did you shoot him, Phillipo?"

"No I didn't shoot the crazy bastard, and they call me Blackie, not Phillipo! I hate that stupid name."

"Okay, Blackie, so why did you shoot your own club member Joey Pazzolino?"

"Fuck you copper! I said I didn't shoot anybody, stop trying to put shit on me I didn't do. I wanna talk to a lawyer if your gonna brow beat me like this!"

The detective turned towards Vito. "Vito why did you shoot Joey?"

"I didn't," Vito stammered.

"Then who did? You, Aldo, did you kill your friend and club member?"

85

"Didn't I just tell you no?" Aldo said calmly, "Oh by the way Brian, I think I'll have one of those cigarettes now."

Detective Gilligan took out a pack of Marlboro Reds tapped the pack and handed a smoke to Aldo. "You're a cool cucumber eh Aldo? King pin of the Black Hawks. You been cruising around with that piece of shit Joey Messina from the Messina clan huh? Now you're a big man?"

"Not so big." said Aldo coolly."

"Big enough to pull a trigger, to show the Messina family that you're capable?"

"Listen you Irish prick, cop or no cop, you're not gonna pin a murder rap on me, especially when I didn't do it!" spit back Aldo.

"Then who did?" Gilligan shouted turning to Vito. "You did it didn't you?!! You snuck up to Joey's apartment and killed him, didn't you! You had marks on your face that day on the sidewalk. We saw them, you struggled with Joey and then shot him in the head! Didn't you?!"

"Fuck you!!" Vito jumped out of his chair. "I didn't do shit, why are you saying that? I didn't do nothing!" He was almost crying with nervous fear.

"You!!" Gilligan turned on Blackie, "were with Vito in the apartment weren't you?"

"No!" said Blackie shaking his head.

"Aldo you set this whole thing up, didn't you? You're the boss, the king pin of the outfit! You set up the murder of Joey because he didn't fit in with your crew any longer, so you sent these two boys," pointing his finger at Vito and Blackie. "You sent these boys to kill Joey Pazzolino, the three of you set this up! I know it and you know it, we all know it. So spill and I will see if I can get you all on Juvenal charges so maybe you'll just get a few years in Jamesburg Reformatory. Spill guys, I got you dead to rights!"

Aldo smiled at the detective. "You got shit man, you got shit and you know it and we all know it. Now I can't talk for these two guys here, but I know that I didn't do a fucking thing, so either book me or release me or let me make a phone call."

"Who are you gonna call Joey Messina?" Gilligan said exasperated.

"It's my business who I call, now either book me or release me!"

"Vito," said the detective, "You did go up to Joeys apartment didn't you?"

Vito following Aldo's lead repeated, "book me or release me!"

Blackie didn't even wait for Gilligan's question. "Book me or release me!" he sneered.

The detective turned his back on them and said "You can go, but I still have questions, I'll see you wise guys again, be sure of that."

The trap was too obvious, the boys were too street wise to fall for the intimidation. However, the cop was not dumb and Vito realized that he would have to be careful. Careful for himself and careful for his brother Dominic.

Walking out of the Police Station, down Washington Ave. Aldo leaned over to Vito and said. "Your little brother shot Joey didn't he?"

Vito froze in his steps, bile came up his chest burning his throat. "What?" he said looking Aldo in the eyes.

"Yeah, the kid spilled it the other day in the candy store. We were busting his balls telling him to go home and put on his big boy pants, and Mikey told him that his balls hadn't dropped yet. Your brother got so mad he told us he had more balls than all of us. We started laughing at him, just busting the kids balls, ya know? That's when the kid spilled it, told us he pulled the trigger on Joey, told us that he'd plug us to if we didn't shut up. At first we thought he was just bullshitting ya know, just a little kid trying to be street an all. But I saw the look in the kids eyes and I knew that he did it." Aldo said nodding his head.

"The kid was just showboating," said Vito nervously. "Ya know, acting like a gangster, he's only little, and where the hell would he get a gat anyway?"

"Wheres your piece?" asked Aldo, looking Vito in the eyes. "Show me your gat[17], now."

"I don't have it on me now." Vito's breath was coming hard. "Why?"

"Fer Christ's sake Aldo we just left the police station, I wasn't gonna carry in there, was I?"

"Yeah, okay V." said Aldo patting Vito's shoulder. "Just want you to know that I'm not gonna say a word, not a peep outta me. But I want you to know that Mikey heard the kid say it too. Mike is stand up and a good Hawk, but I can't vouch for nobody but myself, ya know?"

Vito walked down Monroe street looking at the sidewalk and shaking his head. "Fucking kid, goddamn friggin stupid kid, I told him not to say anything to anybody! Now what are we gonna do? What the hell are we gonna do? If we run, we'll look suspicious. If we stay around, Mikey or even Aldo might spill under pressure. Fucking kid, I swear to God, I don't know what to do now."

As he walked passed 'Turk's Candy Store' Willy looked out of the window. "What's up with you V.?" Asked Willy curiously, "You look upset, what's up?"

"Nothings up, Willy," said Vito, distractedly.

"Come here kid!" Willy yelled, "talk to me."

---

17 Gat --- gun.

"Lasciami solo, per favore. Ho un sacco di cose per la testa. (Leave me alone, I have alot on my mind.") Vito said in Italian.

Vito walked into the apartment through the dining room into the living room where Dominic was watching television. Dominic sat on the sofa engrossed in Spider Man, a cartoon series based on the Marvel comic book character. Vito rushed in on his little brother grabbing him by the hair and pulling him to the floor.

"What the hell are you doing?" Screamed Dominic, struggling to get up.

"What the hell did you do? You stupid little son of a bitch! What did you do?" Vito was shaking Dominic by his hair.

"What, what, what did I do?" he was starting to cry now.

"You told Aldo and Mikey Sabatelli that you offed Joey, that's what you did! After I warned you not to! Now what the hell are we gonna do? They know and if they don't keep their mouths shut everybody will know it. Then they'll take you away and put you in some frigging reformatory for a long time! Momma will die without you and what's Papa gonna say when he gets out?! Meanwhile, I'm an accessory! And I was supposed to look after you! Man, oh man, did you fuck up, Dommie, did you fuck up!"

"I'm sorry, V, I'm sorry!" he was crying now. Tears were running down his flushed cheeks. "They got me mad! They said I was a runt and to go home and all! I just got mad! Listen, I'll wack them; get me a gat and I'll put a bullet in both their heads! I swear, V, I'll get us out of this shit, I will! Just get me another gat!"

Chapter 11

The buzz of conversation ceased as Detective Lieutenant Brian Gilligan walked into the conference room at the Hudson County Police Station. There were approximately ten uniformed policemen and four detectives in the room. They filed into the straight row of seats as Detective Gilligan stood behind the podium on a raised platform. Behind him on the backboards were photographs of Monroe Street. One was an aerial view of the neighborhood, showing the tenements and the quadrant yards and the entrances to the buildings. The other was a drawing of Joey's third floor apartment.

"All right, guys," Gilligan began the discussion, "you all know why we're here. The Mayor and police commissioner have given us orders to break this case. The boys upstairs and the community at large are sick of this gang-related violence and we are positive that this murder is teenage gang involvement."

Gilligan waited for the murmuring to subside before he continued. "Now, what have we got? One tough neighborhood, one murdered teenager and plenty of motives for killing him. He was a crazy, sadistic bully and a key member of the Black Hawks; a feeder gang to the Messina family. I know the kids and they're a tough bunch, I've talked to them, hard nuts to crack everyone of them. I really believe it was the Black Hawks killing one of their own. There are thirty seven known members of this gang all Italian immigrants, close nit and closed mouth, they don't trust the police at all, they look at us as the enemy. Everyone of them are first class suspects."

Gilligan raised his hand, silencing the groans. "I know, it's a tough case, but the Mayor wants the killer. And we've got to find him. So that's why the Commissioner has assigned you men to the case. The killer is probably a kid that's been in here, that we talked to already. There were only fourteen who have been in the reformatory or juvenile court. So now you know what the newspapers know, and we'll go on from there."

"Can we ask questions?" asked one of the patrolmen.

"Anytime, just raise your hand to get my attention. Now let's see what we have already." Gilligan stood up and went to the board. "The kid was killed by one bullet, a 22. Our ballistics show that it was fired by one of those Saturday night specials that these gang members carry. Nothing was taken out of his pockets and nothing was taken out of the apartment, so we're pretty sure that robbery wasn't the motive. Joey Pazzolino had been in a fight and we've got reason to believe that two kids were implicated in the murder instead of one. You see--" Gilligan paused for effect--- "the autopsy shows that Joey had been struck on the back of the head with some sort of weapon, maybe the gun. But the blow wasn't hard enough to knock him out. So he must have been fighting with someone else, from the bruises he had on his face and maybe he was giving some other kid a beating. So we've got two kids to look for. Of course," he went on, "there's always the chance that it was one kid. But we don't think so."

"Did you find out which of the gang were close to him?" Asked one of the Detectives.

"We did," Gilligan said, and took another card from the pile on his desk. "I'll write their names on the board and you can copy them."

When Gilligan finished he turned to the group and said, "You all know that Mikey Sabatelli was a close friend of this Joey Pazzolino, and Vito Fierro and this Phillipo Carrozza, also known as Blackie, were at odds with Joey in some way. At least that's the scuttlebutt on the street. That makes this Vito and Blackie first class suspects. However, they have good alibis."

Gilligan sat on the edge of his desk shaking his head. "You see, what makes this so tough is that none of these kids have prior criminal records yet, and they don't spill the beans on each other. It's like they're still in Sicily and that friggin code of Omerta, that code of silence is so engrained in them that it's like trying to break through centuries of conditioning. It doesn't help that the Messina family lures them in with money and promises of being made men in the Mafia. These feeder gangs are getting wilder and tougher everyday, and our jobs are going to get even tougher, you can count on that."

"You seem pretty pessimistic, Lieutenant," one of the detectives said.

"I know," Gilligan agreed, "but we've got this to go on. I'm sure that two kids knocked off Joey. And I'm willing to go on the premise that Joey knew them. So, first well concentrate on this Black Hawk gang," he pointed to the names of the members listed on the board. "Then we'll work on the others, we're going to raid their clubs. Maybe we'll clue in on something, maybe we won't. Maybe the ones that did it bragged to the guys in their gang, and if we browbeat them maybe one of them will crack. And then," Gilligan shrugged, "we're libel to pick up some kids in the gangs on other charges. Carrying concealed weapons, counterfeit bills, drugs, stuff like that. If we start booking them on these charges, the other gang members just might get disgusted and spill on the killers. Remember, these kids try to look tough, and they hate cops, and they're street savvy. But they're not old enough to know all the ropes. We'll get the killer or killers for that reason. We'll scare them, and in that way well get them.

For over an hour Lieutenant Detective Brian Gilligan led the discussion and oriented the assembled police officers in the physical features of the neighborhood where the murder had taken place. The location of the tenement on Monroe Street and possible entries and exits through the alleyways and quadrants behind the buildings. He stressed again that there were no witnesses who saw or noticed anyone suspicious entering or leaving Joey's apartment building, and that this lack of witnesses complicated the case.

"So there you have it," Gilligan concluded. Now you have all the facts, the first thing to do is to get after this gang. Decide what you need and see Sergeant Tobias, who will keep a record of your activities and get you anything you might need. Good luck."

The four detectives, Sweeney, Thomas, Metcalfe and Fiori, who were assigned to check on the Black Hawks, read the files of all the boys in the gang, quickly noted in the investigation report that Vito Fierro had significant bruise marks on his head and that his little brother looked as if he were in a state of confusion while standing outside their apartment house on the day of the murder.

"They hang out at their club on 7th and Adams Streets," Sweeney read from the report. "I know the area. Pretty tough."

"Used to be a lot of trouble down there in '64 and '65," Metcalfe agreed. "Some of the boys on that block wound up working with the Messina family."

"Why can't we do something about the Messina clan?" said Fiori, they make all us Italians look bad, fucking Sicilians make all Italians look like criminals! Why can't we focus on them instead on a bunch of teenagers? If it weren't for the Messina family feeding these gangs they wouldn't be so prolific."

"The Messina family is the State Police's problem, not ours," said Thomas, "besides, Franco Messina has the Mayor and Commissioner in his pocket, huge payoffs! It's disgusting, even within our own ranks the patrolmen on the beat are paid off to look the other way. They concentrate on the Black and Hispanic gangs and are told to leave the Messina enterprises alone!" Thomas shook his head.

Detective Metcalfe turned and said, "You'd better keep those remarks under your hat, buddy, and just do what you're assigned to do. Never you mind about the Messina family, and you'll retire with your pension. Now, let's concentrate on what we were told to investigate, period! Leave the unmentionable, unmentioned, get it?"

Detective Thomas nodded. "Got it!"

"Good!" said Metcalfe. "Let's get started. Two of us will go down to their club with a wagon picking up as many of the members as we can. And you two," he pointed at Detectives Fiori and Thomas, "pick up the ones hanging out on the corner. Better take some patrolmen with you. How about you coming with me, Sweeney?"

Sweeney nodded, "Okay with me."

"We'll pick them up about ten o'clock tonight," Metcalfe said.

"Let's see," Fiori reached for the report, "they hang out on 7th and Adams Street and on the corner of 4th and Monroe Street at a candy store called 'Turks Palace.' There's a pool room in the back of the store. The neighborhood guys go in and out all night. See you guys tonight. Come on, let's get something to eat," Fiori said to Thomas. "We're gonna be working late tonight."

Chapter 12

Aldo Pinto and Anthony Corizzi were the first ones to notice the patrol wagon coasting to a stop in front of the clubroom. Before they could run, the police had two squad cars up on the sidewalk blocking both sides of the street, completely thwarting any attempt at escape. With speedy efficiency, the police rounded up the boys who vainly tried to run, pushing them roughly into the patrol wagon. The squad cars backed off the sidewalk and followed the wagon back to the police station.

"Alright, out ya go!" A policeman opened the rear door of the wagon. "You guys can unload now, and make it snappy or else you'll get a nightstick across your ass!"

"Big talker," said Mario Cavallo, who immediately received a swift slap across the back of his legs with the officer's nightstick.

"Ouch!!" Mario wailed, hopping up and down from the pain.

"Open your mouth again and see what's next!" Scolded the officer.

"Where's the red carpet for us?" Anthony asked.

"Shut up before you get a slap in the mouth!" The policeman said.

"What are you guys taking us in for?" Aldo asked, "we ain't done nothing, this is harassment, and I for one ain't gonna stand for any of it!"

"Come on, move it along, and keep your mouth shut!" The policeman said impatiently, pushing the boys along with his stick.

Cursing and complaining, the Black Hawks entered the police station and filed onto their assigned benches. They were all a little afraid, for although most of them knew that they had not been implicated in any felony, they were all armed with unregistered pistols and that in itself could mean a stiff sentence.

"Don't answer any questions," Aldo whispered to Anthony, we can ask for lawyers, pass the word."

Anthony winked confidently and passed the word to Vito, who passed it to Mario, who whispered the word to Mikey, who passed it on down the line. Soon, they were all smiling at each other. Aldo began to laugh out loud. This was a big game for them, and to mess with the cops was an even bigger thrill. It showed that they were truly street gangsters and nothing could ruffle them.

"Come on, get seated on those benches!" Detective Metcalfe ordered the Black Hawks who were entering the station, "Listen up, behave until we get to you! Who's the president of the Black Hawks?"

No one spoke.

"Maybe you didn't hear me!" Detective Metcalfe said, annoyed. "Who's the leader?"

"I am," said Aldo, standing up.

Detective Fiori counted rapidly, "We've got seventeen of you hoodlums," he said looking at Aldo, "are all your guys here?"

Aldo laughed, looking at his gang, "all our guys? Officer, we got over thirty guys in our crew. We got more guys on the street than you got bulls in this pen." The other boys started laughing.

The detectives bit their lips in frustration at the enormity of the problem.

Aldo stretched and yawned defiantly. "What you got us here for? We didn't do nuttin. Now, I'm gonna tell you dicks exactly what I always tell ya, book us or release us!"

"Who said you did anything?" Detective Thomas said. "We just want to ask you some questions."

"Suppose we don't talk?" Aldo asked

"Well, we're not going to beat it outta you, but don't worry smart guy, you'll talk, I promise you that." Detective Thomas said.

Aldo chuckled, "You think pretty highly of yourselves, don't ya?"

Detective Metcalfe walked up to Aldo, "Step out here, big shot!"

Aldo didn't move.

Metcalfe pointed to the floor, "Step out, I said, and if you don't step out, that's resisting an officer and I'll drag your guinea ass out! Now move!!" He demanded.

Aldo stepped into the aisle.

"Now, get up front," Detective Metcalfe said, "and put your hands over your head."

Aldo sauntered to the front of the room and slowly raised his hands. He glowered as Detective Thomas went through his pockets, removing his wallet, handkerchief, a wad of bills, small change, cigarettes and a lighter. Thomas ran his hands along Aldo's body looking for a gun.

"Getting a thrill, faggot?" Aldo said, looking at Detective Thomas.

Thomas ignored the insult and, as an afterthought, raised Aldo's trouser legs. There was sheath strapped around his right leg holding a large hunting knife.

Thomas hefted the knife in his hand, "I suppose you use this to clean your fingernails?" he asked Aldo.

"I cut boxes with it," said Aldo.

"Boxes?" Detective Metcalfe said, throwing the Bowie knife on his desk.

"Yeah, I work as a shipping clerk."

"Maybe the judge will believe you," Metcalfe said, mockingly. He called over to one of the patrolmen, "Bremer, book him for carrying a concealed weapon and get him ready for the line-up." He pushed Aldo towards Patrolman Bremer while looking over at the other detectives. "Search them all, every last one of them!"

The Black Hawks were stunned, unable to grasp what was happening. An hour ago they were sitting around the club or hanging on the corner. Now, they were in deep shit. Each one was ordered to the front and searched; as a collection of pistols, knives, brass knuckles and black-jacks grew larger. Only Vito was weaponless but he was still held on suspicion.

Metcalfe called together the other detectives and spoke to them quietly. "We got quite a haul. Did you notice that this kid, Vito Fierro, was the only one not carrying a weapon?"

"Yeah, so what?" said Thomas. "Maybe he just wasn't carrying today."

Detective Metcalfe shook his head. "To be a Black Hawk you have to be armed, it's in their code. These kids may be teenagers but they're none the less gangsters. I want to know why this kid wasn't carrying. I remember that he had bruises on his face the day Joey Pazzolino was killed. I bet you a round of beers that he threw away his piece because it was used!"

The detectives nodded looking at the boys lined up against the wall. Vito stood leaning with his hands in his pockets. Detective Fiori pulled him out of the line. "How come you're not carrying?" He asked.

Vito shrugged, "I didn't want to."

"Don't give me that shit, kid, all you Hawks are supposed to carry. It's in your code."

"What code?" Vito said, smirking.

Detective Thomas grabbed him by the collar, slamming him against the wall. "Your code! The Black Hawks initiation ceremony, you know what I'm talking about! So, don't play stupid with me, kid."

"Fuck you, man!" barked Vito, pushing Detective Fiori off of him. "Get your hands off of me flatfoot!"

Detective Fiori delivered a hard uppercut to his stomach causing Vito to buckle over, then slapped him in the left ear. Vito stumbled sideways and jerked upward. "Go ahead hit me again, you bastard!!" Vito snarled, looking tough in front of his peers. "You're a traitor to our people, an Italian cop! Fuck you, you piece of shit!" Vito spit in Fiori's face. The entire station hushed as Detective Fiori wiped the spittle from his face. A moment hadn't passed when he punched Vito square in the mouth. Blood flowed from the boy's lips as Fiori landed another left hook to the side of his head. Vito fell to the floor as Fiori began kicking him in the ribs in a silent rage.

Metcalfe and Thomas grabbed the enraged detective by the arms pulling him off of the fallen boy. "Enough, enough!!" Yelled Metcalfe, "you're gonna kill him!"

"Fucking A right I'll kill the little bastard!" roared Fiori. "Spit in my face, will ya?!"

Vito slowly and painfully picked himself up off of the floor, while the other Black Hawks looked on. Aldo Pinto started to applaud, the other Hawks following suit. "That's a Black Hawk for ya!" said Aldo. "That Vito can take a trimming from any cop. Good for you, V, good for you!"

"Okay, okay, enough, enough!" Yelled Metcalfe. "Get all these punks booked and take them to their cells. You'd better notify their parents to come down to court tomorrow morning and bail them out.

"Yes sir," said Thomas, "Come on, Fiori, let's book these idiots." With quiet efficiency, the Black Hawks were booked on concealed weapons charges, while Blackie, in addition, was charged for the illegal possession of counterfeit currency. Anthony Corizzi was charged with a narcotic violation in addition to carrying a 22. caliber pistol. Vito was booked on suspicion and for resisting arrest by putting his hands on Detective Fiori.

As they all sat in their cells they did not speak to one another. For playing at being a gangster and putting one over on the cops was fun. Now they were facing serious charges and possible reformatory time. The bravado, the scowling sneer, the eye to eye contact that was supposed to scare the cops hadn't worked.

Detective Metcalfe brought Vito into a private room. "Okay, kid, why don't you have a gat on you?"

"I don't own one! I told you that already."

"Bullshit, kid, all you Hawks carry gats, it's mandatory. You think I don't know that. No knife or knuckles, no weapons at all? It don't make sense."

Vito's hands were sweaty. He felt as if the walls of the room were closing in on him, squeezing him until there was no breath left in his body. Detective Metcalfe noticed his nervousness and pressed the issue. A street wise detective such as Metcalfe could smell his fear.

"Come on kid," pressed Metcalfe. What are you hiding? Who are you protecting? I can see that you're hiding something! You were the only guy out there without a weapon on you, why? Seems like you're scared to carry for some reason."

Vito screwed up his face and began to fake sobbing. He didn't want to do it; crying was pussy shit, but he had to. Now his mind was clear and ticking like a clock. As much as he feared and hated the police, he had to admit they had him. With every muscular reflex, he compelled himself to cry. Finally, as a release from the tension, the tears came in a torrent of emotion.

Lieutenant Brian Gilligan walked in looking at Vito, shaking his head in disgust and annoyance. "Snap out of it, kid! We're letting you go! So, turn off the fake water works and get out of here!"

"You're not booking me?" asked Vito, looking at Gilligan.

"No! Now go home! But I want you to know I'm not buying any of your bullshit, fake tears and all! I've been around the block a few times myself! I know your dirty! I know you know something about this murder! So, just understand that this isn't over, not by a long shot! Now, get the hell outta here before I change my mind!"

"What about the other guys?" asked Vito, looking concerned.

"They're booked."

"No! They'll think that they're taking the rap for me!"

"I guess your friends aren't gonna like you too much, huh?"

"Why can't you give them a break? I swear on my mother and father, they never done nothing!" begged Vito, starting to tear up.

"Here we go again," said Detective Metcalfe, looking at Gilligan. "This kid should be in Hollywood, he's some actor."

"Let them go," begged Vito! "They'll have it in for me! They'll think I'm a rat!"

"Maybe we could strike a deal?" Detective Gilligan suggested.

Vito was suspicious, "Like what?"

"Tell us who shot and killed Joey Pazzalino."

"I told you already, I don't know," moaned Vito, shaking his head and looking at his feet. "I don't know!"

Detective Gilligan looked at the other detectives sighing, "This meeting is adjourned!" he opened the door saying to Vito, "Go home and stay out of trouble!"

Vito's eyes were red, his face was drawn and pale as he left the police station. The stress and fear of almost being discovered drained and weakened him to the point where he could barely walk home.

As Vito was leaving the police station, he saw Father Joe sitting in the waiting room with his mother and his brother Dominic.

"What did they want?" Vito's mother asked him."

"They wanted to know who killed Joey."

"Why did they ask you? What does my son know about such things?" Vito's mother begged for an answer, looking at Father Joe helplessly.

"Ma, I don't know what these cops are thinking! They're driving me nuts!"

"And what happened to your face?" Vito's mother asked looking at her son concerned. "You look all beaten up, did they hit you?"

"Forget it ma," said Vito. "It's okay!"

"But your face, it's all swelled!" She said staring at him.

"I said forget, ma, so just forget it, okay!"

"Let's get some coffee," said Father Joe. "We'll go to Shaffer's diner and get a little something to eat; it's on me." He took Vito's mother's arm guiding her out of the station. "I've got my car outside. After we have some refreshments, I'll drive you home. Come on, boys, he said kindly to Vito and Dominic; let's go."

"These cops are scaring the hell outta me!" said Vito, nervously.

"Don't worry," said Father Joe. "Tomorrow I'll straighten things out for you. Come on now, lets go and have something to eat."

Mrs. Fierro opened the door of the automobile looking at Father Joe. "What am I gonna do Father? My husband is in jail. I have to work every day and every night just to keep food on the table and pay the rent," she sobbed, as the boys slid into the back seat of the Ford Galaxy.

Father Joe sighed, as he turned the ignition key on. "I don't know, Mrs. Fierro. This thing is way over my head." He turned to Vito and Dominic saying, "Do you boys know anything about this?"

Vito looked at Dom while Dom looked at him. They both shook their heads, "No, we don't Father!"

"Mother Mary, help me!" Mrs. Fierro said, looking up at the sky. "First, we are poor because we don't have no money. Now my poor husband is in jail and my two boys have no one to look after them." She grabbed Vito's arm pleadingly, "Tell me you're not in trouble!"

"I'm not!" said Vito, roughly. "Now stop bothering me, will ya!"

Father Joe coasted to a stop in front of Shaffer's Diner. "Leave him alone, Mrs. Fierro. He's had enough interrogation for one day. Come on, people, let's get out."

Mrs. Fierro and Dominic entered the diner first. Father Joe whispered to Vito, "Lucky thing you got rid of that gun; good thing you listened to me."

"Yeah, thanks," said Vito, walking past Father Joe into the diner.

Father Joe grabbed Vito by the arm. "You're a first class suspect and I've got a feeling that you're not telling everything you know. Remember, Vito, talking to the police might save you a lot of grief later on."

Vito sneered as he sat in the booth with his mother and brother. Except for his red rimmed eyes and the lines that furrowed his brow, he was cold and distant. The cops were stupid. Father Joe was stupid. The Black Hawks were stupid. All he had to do was think and he could outsmart everyone. The only hitch was that Dominic had opened his mouth to Aldo and Mickey. Other than that, nobody knew anything and what they didn't know couldn't hurt him. Vito leaned over to Father Joe and whispered, "Nobody is asking you for advice!"

Chapter 13

For Vito, July meant one more month of dread. The fear of being discovered consumed his mind. He constantly thought of escaping New Jersey and heading west; Wyoming, Colorado, Nebraska, any place but Hoboken, New Jersey, where he could be found out. However, he didn't have the financial means to leave or the mental acuity to actually plan an escape. He knew that that prick Mickey had it in for him and that he could squeal on him at any time. He wanted to protect his mother and little brother from experiencing any more unnecessary grief. He was jumpy and paranoid believing that everyone was conspiring against him. Now as he walked down Washington Avenue with Angela, her beguiling chatter made no impression on him.

He could not rest or be at ease, since it was only a week after they had killed Joey and he had almost been trapped by the police. Maybe, he thought, it would have been better to have been caught. Then this constant wariness and tension which were sapping his strength and refusing him the relaxation of sleep would cease. Wherever he went, he would see Detectives Metcalfe or Gilligan or some other flatfoot following him, looking at him. If he went into the candy store, Detective Metcalfe would be sitting there drinking coffee and would invite him to sit at his table. The talk made Vito nervous. His jaw would stiffen, his hands would sweat and his legs would bounce uncontrollably. He knew that the direction of Metcalfe's talk was meant to catch him in some contradiction, or a flaw in his alibi. One day he walked into Shaffer's Diner with Angela. They saw Detective Gilligan sitting at the counter noisily sucking a chocolate egg cream through a straw. They wanted to leave immediately but Detective Gilligan insisted on buying them sodas and talking. Gilligan spoke only of the murder and police theory about what had happened; what Vito thought of how it might have occurred. Vito just shook his head while looking at Angela and shrugging his shoulders making sure to give nothing away.

Detective Gilligan said that he felt the murder was not premeditated and that the boy would receive mercy from the court if he confessed. "Yeah," said Gilligan, "maybe the kid that did it wants to confess, but maybe someone else is implicated in the killing and one guy can't confess because of the other guy. We feel that there were two guys in the apartment when Joey was killed. What do you think?" He asked Vito.

"Listen," Vito said, "I told you guys a million times already, I don't know nothing about this shit. What are you trying to do anyway, put me in the middle of this mess? I got nothing to do with it and that's that! Now, stop harassing me, I'm sick of this crap!"

"Yeah, well, so am I kid, so am I," Gilligan said, sucking on his straw. He got up and left the diner.

After he left, Vito and Angela sat silently looking at each other. "Do you know anything about this?" Asked Angela, searching Vito's face for the truth.

"What are you a cop, too?" Vito barked at her. "Why the fuck is everybody asking me about this shit! Just because I lived next door to that crazy bastard, Joey, I somehow know what happened? Just everybody leave me alone!" He got up and walked out of the diner, leaving Angela sitting in the booth.

Detectives Metcalfe, Gilligan, and the other detectives were everywhere on Monroe Street, Adams Street, Jackson Street and strolling in front of the Black Hawk's club room. They always stopped and talked to Vito, or Aldo or any of the other gang members; asking the same questions over and over again, playing a sort of game whereby they seemingly wanted their opinions about the murder. Vito suddenly realized, with terror, that the police had eliminated practically every boy in the gang. He was the only one left that Detective Gilligan continued to ask about the murder.

To make matters worse, the story broke in the newspapers that the Black Hawks had been picked up by the police and all but Vito were being held on various charges. Their landlord made them move out of their club room on Adams Street. In a vicious vengeance, the Hawks had poured quick drying cement down the toilet and sink ruining the plumbing. They ruined the flooring by spilling melted tar on the parquet. They then warned the landlord that his body would be found floating in the river, if he made a complaint. Now, the Black Hawks had no meeting place. This, coupled with the fact that they were all out on bail facing prosecution, made them turn on Vito as a direct cause of their present persecution.

Mikey stopped Vito in front of Turks Candy store pulling him into an adjacent alleyway. His face was red with rage as he grabbed Vito by the collar telling him that he knew he and his little brother Dominic were responsible for the murder. Now, on charges of gun and drug possession, he was facing a prison rap.

"Every dime I had in the bank," he tersely spit at Vito, "and plenty of my old man's money. We had to give it a lawyer who thinks he can get me off. And, it's all your fault!" He refused to let

Vito speak. "You can tell the cops that you don't know who bumped off Joey but I know what your little brother told me. And because you're keeping your mouth shut to save your brother's ass, I might go to the can!"

Vito looked at him in disbelief, "What, are you gonna rat us out!! You took an oath never to squeal on a Black Hawk brother!! What do you want me to do, turn myself and my brother in?!"

"I don't know what I want!" Mikey cried in exasperation. "But I gotta get this rap off my neck! You know I could go to Rahway Prison for five years on this rap!"

"You'll beat it," said Vito, not really believing his prediction.

"What's the use of talking to you!" Mikey said accusingly, "You got us into this mess by wacking Joey! Now look, the entire club has charges against us, all except you! Why is that Vito?! Why is it that only you don't have charges against you?"

"You know why, 'cause I was the only one not carrying a gat that day!"

"And why not?! You always carry! We all carry, that's the rules! We were all carrying, but you! So, we all got charged with concealed weapons and drugs while you walked away clean! You know I know the truth!"

"You don't know shit! You're a fucking asshole! You better keep your mouth shut, or else!" said Vito, moving in on Mikey.

"Why, what the hell are you gonna do anyway?!" said Mikey, grabbing Vito by the collar in a fit of rage. Vito brought up a knee smashing Mikey in the groin. Mikey bent over in shock and pain as Vito came down with an elbow on the back of his neck. He collapsed on the pavement as Vito kicked him viciously in the ribs with his pointed shoes. Snatching him up by his hair, Vito snarled in his face; "You motherfucker! You squeal on me and you're a dead man, understand?! A fucking dead man!" He let him go, spitting on him as he exited the alleyway.

Chapter 14

Once the detectives visited Angela and Anna, questioning them about the murder, Anna would no longer date Blackie. Angela continued to see Vito, although they didn't have Blackie's car to cruise around in anymore. Blackie was cold to Vito since the bust.

As Vito walked with Angela along Washington Avenue, the summer night was cool and pleasant. He was silent and only dimly aware of her presence.

"You're ignoring me," Angela pouted, pressing Vito's arm.

"Vito put his arm around her waist. "I'm sorry, sweetie, I was just thinking."

"Thinking so much that you haven't even kissed me?"

Vito pulled her close and kissed her softly on the lips.

"Not here, in front of everybody, you nut!" Angela laughed. " You're kissing me right here on Washington Ave., in public? What are we Gypsies?"

Vito laughed as they turned left onto Fourth Street walking down to Fifth Street Park. He guided her from the path to an enclosed thicket of bushes near the big gazebo. He knelt feeling the grass.

"It's dry, Angela," he said, removing his jacket. "We'll sit on this," he said, spreading his jacket on the ground.

"That's a new suit," she protested.

"What the hell's the difference?" Vito lay on his back with his hands locked behind his head. "Come on, sit next to me."

Angela cupped his face in her hands and kissed him. "Feel better now?" she whispered seductively.

His reply was to pull her on top of him kissing her gently on the lips. "I wouldn't know what to do without you," he whispered back to her. "I really wouldn't know what to do."

Again she kissed him, finally relaxing, laying beside him stroking his chest, feeling the muscles tense under his shirt. As his free hand caressed her neck, breasts, and her thighs.

"I love you, Vito," Angela's voice was heavy with passion as his hand slipped under her dress. "I love you more than anything!" She took his hand and pressed it between her legs moaning with desire, passion and the magic of a warm summer evening.

Vito kissed her neck as he moved his hand up and down between her legs. She sighed, "Vito, what are you waiting for?"

"Here?" he said, looking around the park.

"We're all alone and I'm dying for you!" Her nails dug through his shirt. "We're all alone, you know, and I never asked anyone before." She trembled in his arms with a desire she could no longer control.

Vito rolled over looking down upon her as she lay with her hair flowing and her eyes half shut. He kissed her again and again, fully, wildly, consuming her with a hunger that had been held back for too long. Neither one held back their desire as a scintillating series of ecstatic reflexes released their passion.

Sighing they relaxed and listened to the night sounds of the city multiplying all around them. The circle of hedges hid them as they lie in a private world all their own. Angela laid on her side hugging Vito. As she kissed him, he continued to stare at the night sky.

"V," she said softly, "It's late."

He raised his left arm and looked at his watch. "It's almost twelve. That was never late for me before, but now I have to get home early to avoid those damn detectives," he said bitterly.

Angela sat up and stroked his hair. "Don't let them bother you," she tried to console him. "It'll all be over soon. They're bound to get the ones who did it."

Vito's throat tightened when she said that the police were bound to find out who did it. He was glad that it was dark so she couldn't see the fear twisting his face. "Why do you say that?" he asked.

"Well, the police are pretty efficient. You never see in the papers or on the news that a murder hasn't been solved. It's only a matter of time."

"But they haven't any clues," he said, swallowing nervously.

"Oh, how do you know?" she giggled, kissing his nose. "Do you think they let out all their information? I mean they're professionals. This is what they do all day every day. Believe me, they'll find out who killed Joey, don't you worry."

Vito shoved her away, "Shut up now, will ya? You sound like that friggin Detective Metcalfe or that other prick, Gilligan. They pop up everywhere I go. They're driving me nuts!" Vito rolled over and lay with his face in his folded arms.

"I'm sorry I brought it up baby," Angela spoke softly, as she rubbed his head. "Come on, you better take me home now. Oh, V," she embraced him as she stood up, "I think I'm falling in love with you."

"I think I'm falling in love with you, too." Vito replied sincerely, as he brushed the loose grass from her skirt. He lifted his jacket from the grass, putting it on and brushed his hair back casually. "Let's go."

Angela held his arm as they walked so that their thighs rubbed together. "You sure are a great lover," she said shyly as their eyes met. "What's wrong?" Vito halted abruptly, rigid with panic.

"That man ahead of us looks like one of the detectives," he whispered, chewing his lower lip in apprehension. "Let's go back!"

"No!" she insisted, "and even if it is, if you run you'll look suspicious, come on!" she dragged him along the side walk. "We'll walk fast and pass him. It's probably not even him, calm down."

Shaking, Vito allowed himself to be led. As they approached the man who was strolling ahead of them he realized that it was neither Metcalfe, Gilligan or any of the other detectives. He realized that he was seeing them even when they were not present. He had to snap out of it. He knew that his nerves were frazzled, stretched to the point of snapping.

"See," Angela said to him after they passed the man. "It wasn't one of them after all, was it?"

They walked up to Washington Avenue without speaking. Vito turned to Angela, "Look babe, how about I put you in a cab and I'll walk home?"

Before she could protest, Vito whistled sharply at a passing Hudson Cab which stopped suddenly, grinding its gears as the driver stepped on the brakes. Vito opened the door and pushed Angela inside.

"How much to the Marion Section of Jersey City?" Vito asked the driver.

The driver looked tired, "It's about two dollars."

Vito handed him a five. "Take this girl home. Bye sweetie," he leaned in giving her a kiss on the lips. "I'll call you tomorrow."

Angela kissed him back. "Good night, please don't worry about anything. Everything is going to be alright. I love you."

"Love you too," said Vito as he shut the cab door.

Vito watched as the cab drove away; then walked into a drugstore near the Hudson tubes, (subway). He entered the store's phone booth to call Father Joe. Why he wanted to talk to Father Joe he could not explain. But, in Father Joe he sensed a person who was willing and anxious to help him. Although the hope was a faint one, possibly Father Joe could suggest an escape from the secret that oppressed him. Vito felt no guilt about Joey Pazzo. He did feel anger towards his brother Dominic for spilling his guts to Aldo and Mikey; enabling them to hold this terrible secret over their heads. He had just beat up Mikey. He wondered if the son of a bitch would now turn him in for spite. Maybe instead of talking to Father Joe, he should talk to Aldo Pinto and have him remind Mikey of his oath to never turn a brother Hawk into the authorities. In his mind, there were some schemes to consider: like throwing the onus of suspicion on a few negro boys in his high school class by making an anonymous phone call to the police. He could tell them that Joey was killed by some niggers in the Pagans gang. Or, blame it on one of the Puerto Rican kids that they had beaten up a few weeks before. However, he had to reject every scheme because he could not fill in the necessary details to make the new angle appear believable. He ran his finger down the row of telephone numbers in the phonebook; there it was, Saint Ann's Parish telephone number.

"Hi Father Joe, it's me, Vito Fierro. I know it's late but I have to talk to you. Is it okay if I come over to the rectory?"

Father Joe had sleep in his voice but his answer was, "Come right over son, I'll be waiting."

Vito walked up to the the rectory door, hesitantly. The door opened and Father Joe stood there smiling. "Come in, Vito. I'm so glad that you decided to talk to me. Even though it's twelve a.m., I'm glad you came by," he said, putting his hand on Vito's shoulder while leading him into the rectory parlor.

Vito wrung his hands. "I'm sorry I disturbed you, Father," he said, lowering his eyes. "I woke you up, didn't I?"

"It's all right." Father Joe shook his head and lit a lamp that stood on an end table in the parlor. "Sit down," he went on, "take off your jacket if you want to, I'll be back in a minute. I'm going to wash my face to wake me up."

Vito sat on the sofa, nervously taking off his suit jacket. He squatted down to look at the selection of books on Father Joe's book shelf. But as he heard the door open, he sat up sitting stiffly on the sofa.

"You usually come visiting at this hour?" asked Father Joe, smiling.

"I don't know what made me come here, Father."

"Do you want to have a cup of coffee with me?" Father Joe asked.

"I guess so."

"Come with me to the kitchen while I put on a pot."

Vito stood in the doorway as Father Joe put the coffee pot to perk on the stove. He took out some biscuits from the cabinet setting them down on the table. "Come sit," he motioned Vito. "Now, what's on your mind, son, as if I didn't know."

"What do you know?" said Vito, defensively.

"I know that you wouldn't be coming here after midnight if you weren't in some sort of trouble."

Vito grasped his knees to keep them from trembling. "I didn't do nothing, Father, nothing I tell ya, nothing!"

Father Joe got up and poured two cups of coffee. "You didn't do anything? Then, what's the problem?"

113

"Everyone's down on me."

"That's not hard to understand."

"Great, a lot of help you are Father. Maybe I shouldn't have come here."

Father Joe wrinkled his forehead, "Help? It seems to me that I offered you help more than once. What do you expect me to do? Do you expect me to keep offering it to you as though it's a free pass to a movie? You're in a spot, Vito. The cops are smart. Remember you were the only one they found weaponless. And on the day that Joey was killed you had bruise marks all over your face and head. Did you think that that went unnoticed by the police?"

Vito did not look at him. "I threw the gun away like you told me to."

"Before or after Joey was killed?"

Vito wearily rubbed his hands over his face. "Before, Honest, before."

"Would you like to receive the Sacrament of Confession, Vito?" Father Joe offered.

Vito shook his head, saying, "I burnt a holy card in my hands while giving an oath that I would burn in hell if I revealed any of the activities of the Black Hawks."

Father Joe put his hand on Vito's hand. "God forgives all, Vito. There is nothing that you could ever do to make him turn his back on you."

"You're a good guy, Father," Vito said, smiling sadly.

"Thank you, I would like the chance to help you."

Vito did not reply.

"Come on,"Father Joe bit into a biscuit and took a sip of coffee. "We've been dancing around for too long. What did you come here for?"

"I don't know why I came!"

"Who killed Joey Pazzolino?"

Vito threw the biscuit back on the plate, "I don't know!"

"You are not telling the truth!" Father Joe insisted. "Who are you protecting? I know that the detectives are on to you. I see them prowling the neighborhood. Two of them came to see me probing about you and your brother."

"My brother? Why the hell would they ask about a ten year old kid? What the hell does he know?"

"They saw the two of you standing on the sidewalk the day Joey was killed. You looked as though you had just taken a beating. They related to me that Dominic looked as though he were in a daze. So you tell me what happened. Come on V, I know you know something."

Vito clutched the table. "What did the cops want to know?"

"The usual things; what I thought of you and did I think you shot Joey."

"Why the hell would I shoot Joey? He was a member of my club! He was a friend of mine, we hung together! What did you tell the cops about me?" Vito was frantic as he looked at Father Joe.

"I told them that I didn't think you had killed anybody. Now, I never mentioned your gun."

"I threw it away! I swear to God, Father, I threw the gun in the river!"

"I believe you, Vito, don't get so upset. Sit down and drink your coffee. I understand that you're scared."

Vito's cup dropped, as he suddenly bolted up. "Scared?! Scared of what?! Who said that I'm scared?!"

Father Joe stirred his coffee idly, "I don't know, something that brought you here after twelve o'clock midnight."

"I'm leaving!" said Vito, shoving back his chair.

"Sit down!"Father Joe ordered him. "We're going to talk this out. I know you're going to tell me there's nothing to talk about. All right, then I'm asking you again, why did you come here tonight?"

Vito was silent. Slowly, he picked up a biscuit and dunked it in his coffee.

"Come on, man," Father Joe insisted, "you're wasting my time and yours. Tell me what's wrong and I'll try to help." He tried another tactic. "They picked up Louie Morella and Frankie Natoli from the Bristol Boys."

Vito nodded, "I know them, the cops raided their club. So what?"

"I talked with Louie Morella and Frank Natoli, they're out on bail for concealed weapons charges. And you know what?"

"What?"

"They're not scared. They're angry that the cops busted their club but they're not scared. You my friend are terrified! Why?"

Vito looked at him stonefaced. "What, now I'm supposed to tell you that I'm scared when I'm not!"

Father Joe blew at the hot coffee. "What are you scared of?"

"Nothing! Not a fucking goddamn thing!"

"Don't use that foul language in front of me, young man!" Father Joe yelled, standing up authoritatively. "Then, why did you come here?!"

"I, I,---"

"Say it!"

Vito's lips clamped together. It would be so easy, so tempting, to tell Father Joe everything. He knew Father Joe would try to help him, but there was his little brother Dominic and the Black Hawks to consider. No matter how mad Mikey was at him for taking a rap and getting a beating; Vito didn't believe that Mikey would rat out a brother Black Hawk. Detectives Gilligan and Metcalfe were in the dark and fishing, he knew that. What he had was a case of the jitters.

He was worrying too much about getting caught. All he had to do was stop worrying and chill out.

Now he had Angela, and she was wonderful. She was better than any girl he had ever had before. The best thing was that she actually loved him. Angela thought he was the greatest guy in the world. She was beautiful, Italian, sexy, smart; the kind of girl that any one of the Hawks would give their right arm for and she was all his.

He was sure he could somehow straighten this mess out. Once school started, he would go to class everyday. He promised himself he would study and get decent grades. He would see Angela at night and make love to her. Sure, he was just nervous. All this shit would pass. He just had to be cool, he told himself.

"Well?" said Father Joe, sharply.

"Good biscuits Father," he sniggered while dunking one in his coffee.

"So, that's your attitude?"

"No attitude, I just stopped by to say hello."

"And you expect me to believe that," said Father Joe, getting angrier by the minute.

"Nobody's asking you what to believe or not believe. I'm just having a cup of coffee."

Father Joe picked up a biscuit crumpling it in his hand. He had an overwhelming urge to slap Vito in the face. "You don't have to tell me anything, Vito! But I know that you are being watched! You know it too and it's easy to see that it's getting to you. Now, suppose the detectives saw you come in here at twelve midnight? They would surmise that you were scared and came here to tell me what you know or did!"

"I didn't do anything!" Vito saw the walls of the kitchen shift and waver as if they were about to fall on him.

"So, you didn't do anything?" Father Joe went on relentlessly, battering the walls that Vito had erected. "The cops will again question me. I'll tell them that I don't know anything, because in reality I don't! I won't even tell them what I suspect."

"What? What do you suspect?" Vito struggled to talk, as he placed his hand against the wall to steady himself.

"What do you think I suspect?" asked Father Joe.

"If the cops ask you anything, you tell them that I came to ask you for advice because they were making me so miserable."

Father Joe shook his head. "You haven't asked my advice."

"That's what you tell them!" Vito hissed, "You tell them that my mother is making it hard for me because the cops are harassing us so much. I didn't do a damn thing to anyone! Do you understand, Father?! You tell them what I tell you to tell them if you know what's good for you!"

"I see, you want me to lie for you."

"You better!" Vito stood pressing his knuckles into the table. "I'm not taking nobody's rap for murder when I didn't do a fucking thing!!! I didn't kill Joey, I swear!"

"And your brother Dominic?" Father Joe stared Vito in the eyes. "Dominic has been telling the kids in school that he's a killer and that he's made his bones."

"He's a friggin little kid! He's just playing a mob guy 'cause he thinks it's cool. He's a kid, a ten year old kid. I look after him, it was my responsibility." Vito turned and walked out of the kitchen. "I'm leaving, Father, thanks for the coffee." Vito's hands were shaking as Father Joe handed him his jacket.

"I'm sorry I bothered you, Father. I'll be seeing you around."

"Father Joe held open the door. "Goodnight, sleep well if you can sleep at all."

Vito tried to wave casually but concern and fear made the flippant gesture weak. "I will, goodnight. Thanks for the coffee and biscuits."

Chapter 15

The days dragged on endlessly as the Black Hawks refused to acknowledge Vito's existence. At first, it didn't bother him because he figured that this was his chance to get loose from the gang. But now he had nowhere to go. He was a marked man all over the neighborhood. He was seen as a rat or at least someone who had gotten the rest of the Hawks in big trouble.

Vito was trying with everything he had to protect his little brother. But the kid was bragging and shooting his stupid mouth off. It was Dominic, always Dominic, with his adolescent yakking. Vito was going crazy trying to get the kid to keep his mouth shut. So, when Aldo called him into Turk's Candy Store for a meeting, he tried to appear calm but his heart was throbbing in his chest. As he walked into the candy store, he saw Aldo and Blackie sitting in a booth.

He slid into the booth across from Aldo, "I got your message," Vito said, "What's up?"

"The club is running a dance," said Aldo.

"A dance?" said Vito, confused.

"Yeah, a dance," said Blackie, nodding his head. "We're raising money to help our members with their legal bills that came from this friggin bust! We all got charges against us, except you!" he said, frowning at Vito. "So, we're running a dance!"

Aldo reached into his jacket removing a thick envelope, which he placed on the table. "Here's the tickets," he explained. "We're running this dance two weeks from tomorrow night to raise money for the Black Hawks." He looked Vito squarely in the eyes. "All of us guys need the dough. Not everyone has a bank account, ya know. So we figured, we would run this dance and raise money. We printed a thousand tickets."

"A thousand tickets?!" Vito exclaimed incredulously. "Where are you gonna run this dance?!"

"Every guy needs two tickets to get in with his date," said Aldo, ignoring Vito's question. "And, the tickets cost ten bucks a piece."

Vito's mouth dropped opened. "You mean you're gonna get guys to shell out twenty bucks for a dance?!" Where are ya holding it?"

Aldo smiled smugly, "I talked with Joey Messina. He's letting us use the Union Club on Hudson Street. He's a swell guy." Aldo nodded knowingly, "I'm getting close with the Messina family. They're good people. They're gonna make sure the other clubs know that they're behind us. I'm sure we'll sell out our tickets."

"You gotta be crazy!" Vito objected. "How the hell are you gonna fit a thousand people in the Union Club?!"

Aldo took two tickets out of the envelope and handed one each to Vito and Blackie. "Look at the beautiful printing job," said Aldo. "We got it for nuttin. This dance is gonna be all profit. We don't even have to pay for the fuckin hall. The Messina family is covering everything for us."

"Really?" Blackie said, "Why are they doing this for us?"

Aldo smirked, "'Cause, I'm in with them big time. Eventually, I'll take the oath; then I'll be a Messina. Believe you me, then you'll see the money rolling in. He nodded his head again, smiling. "They're helping us out big time!"

"Great!" said Vito. "But I still don't see how you're gonna fit a thousand people in the hall."

"Look at the tickets," chided Aldo. "See what it says about not coming before nine o'clock? Some of the tickets say nine o'clock, some say ten o'clock, some say eleven, some say twelve. The tickets are on different colored paper for different times. When the couples come in, they have to pin their tickets to their suits and dresses so we can see them. The Messina family are gonna supply us with some real gorillas who are gonna watch the door and act as bouncers in case there's any trouble. A couple with a ten o'clock ticket can only get in between ten and one minute to eleven. These hard guys will be circulating on the floor. When they see the place is getting too crowded, they'll go to the couples who have been there the earliest and kick them out. This way the crowd will keep changing and we won't have a mob scene."

"Who are the hard guys?" asked Blackie.

"Like I said, some guys from the Messina clan. These guys are hard!" He said, pounding his fist in his hand. "No one and I mean no one is gonna argue with these guys!"

Aldo glanced over at Blackie. "Listen, step outside for a minute. I gotta talk with Vito in private."

Blackie got up without question walking out to the sidewalk to smoke a cigarette.

Aldo leaned across the table staring intensely into Vito's eyes. "Look, V, you know that I know the truth about you and your brother, Dominic."

"Yeah," Vito nodded, nervously.

"Well, I want you to know, I ain't no rat. I ain't gonna say shit to nobody. And, I'm gonna make sure that Mikey don't say shit either. Listen, up, V, Mikey is sore as hell at you for knocking the crap outta him the other day. He want's to get even with you in the worst way."

"So, what?! He want's to rat me out to the cops?!"

"That ain't gonna happen," said Aldo, "not on my watch. You know I'm getting real close with Joey Messina. To tell you the truth, I'm probably eventually gonna take the oath, ya know? You know the way the Messina family feels about rats. If they even suspect that somebody ratted out a guy for stealing a slice of gum, he's shit to them. So nobody and I mean nobody from the Hawks is ratting out anybody as long as I'm in charge, *capisci (understand)?*"

Vito nodded, "So, I'm jake[18] with the Hawks again?"

Aldo nodded, "Yeah, you're jake. Ya don't have to worry about Mikey turning you in. Now, if he hits you in the back of the head with a bat, that's none of my business, but he ain't gonna rat, that's for sure!"

Aldo turned to the door and whistled for Blackie to come back in. Blackie slid into the booth next to Vito. Aldo handed them each an envelope. "I'm giving you guys thirty tickets each. That's ten dollars a ticket. I want you to sell all of them. That's three hundred from each of you! Every dollar we take in counts, so no skimming dough off the top!"

Vito shook his head doubtfully, "Thirty tickets, are you sure this is gonna go over?"

"What's the matter, V?" Said Aldo, leaning across the table. "Not enough? Maybe you want forty?"

---

18 Jake, street slang for Okay cr back in good graces.

"Stop fucking with me!" Vito said, pushing his face forward to meet Aldo's stare. "I can ask questions. If I'm supposed to take thirty, I'll take them, but don't practice being a hard guy on me!"

Aldo stood to his full height. He leaned across the table glowering menacingly at Vito. "Who do you think you're talking to?!" He seethed through clenched teeth.

"Cut it out, both of you," Blackie said. "We got enough trouble already. You can get rid of thirty tickets, V, and it's for a good cause. The guys are struggling with legal fees and all. We're gonna divide the money according to who needs it the most."

Aldo calmed down. "Okay, you're right." He looked at Vito. "Just remember who you're talking to. I'm doing you a solid just letting you back in the Hawks."

"I suppose," nodded Vito, "you don't need to get in my face, that's all. I'll take the thirty tickets."

"Let me write down the numbers on your tickets," said Aldo to Vito. "You got a ten o'clock batch so they should be easy to sell." He counted out another thirty tickets handing them to Blackie. "This'll be your thirty, make sure you sell all of them. They should sell fast. Hit the streets, go to all the stores, the clubs, everybody. Let them know that the Messina family is behind this thing. They'll be afraid not to buy a ticket or two. Joey Messina is gonna come with his girl including all the cousins and associates; they promised me. People will come just to be in good with them."

Is that asshole Ronnie Messina gonna be there?" asked Blackie. "I hate that fuck! He thinks he's a tough guy, waving that straight razor around all the time."

Aldo looked at Blackie, "Just watch who you're talking about, if you know what's good for ya."

"Word on the street is that Tony Messina kicked the shit out of his cousin Ronnie just before he went in the Army," Vito chimed in.

Aldo balked impatiently, "Listen you two, did you hear me say shut the fuck up about the Messina Family?! If you say anything at all, you say good shit, understand? Only talk about how Don Franco gives out turkeys and hams on Christmas or how he'll help you out of a jam if you ask him."

"Yeah, well he's not helping us out of this jam with the police, is he?" said Blackie.

"No?! He's not?! The Messina's are paying for this whole fucking dance for us! The money will go to the club to help out the guys who need it! What the fuck is that?! Isn't that helping us out of a jam?! Now, again, shut the hell up before I slap both of you in the mouth!"

Vito looked at the tickets which had been assigned to him, counting them, and putting them in his jacket pocket. "Who gets the money?" he asked.

"I do!" Aldo replied, emphatically.

"You know what Tony Corizzi is doing?" Blackie interjected.

"What?" Vito asked.

"His arrest rap is costing him plenty. So, he went out and had raffle tickets printed up. He's raffling off a Panasonic color T.V. set."

"Hey, that's a good idea," said Vito.

"But the funny part is," Blackie laughed, "The tickets don't say where the raffle is gonna be held or the date. So, he just keeps the money. He hasn't even bought a T.V. set!"

Aldo roared, "That's Tony for ya, a real Sicilian."

"Hey," Vito laughed, "I got one for ya. I know a guy who's half Jewish and half Sicilian, if he can't get it for you wholesale, he steals it!"

Aldo laughed. "Yeah, they say us Siggies[19] are thieves, but we never steal from the average guy, just, ya know, trains and big stores and shit like that. That's not really stealing. We're not like the niggers and spics who rob peoples houses, ya know?"

The guys nodded in agreement. "Yeah," said Blackie, "we're much better than niggers and spics. We're Italian and that's the best!"

Chapter 16

Vito found that selling the thirty tickets was not too difficult, for the Black Hawks were the first to plan a dance that summer. When Vito told prospective customers that the money was going to be used to keep the Black Hawks out of jail, they sold steadily. Some boys who were reluctant to part with twenty dollars for two tickets had only to be reminded that there were many dark streets in Hoboken; and guys were occasionally held up and beaten by unknown thugs--- and more tickets were sold.

Vito opened his collar and loosened his tie as he walked up the steps of his building. Aldo now insisted that all the Hawks wear a suit and tie when walking around. This was a new development since Aldo was making inroads with the Messina family. Mobsters wore suits so the Black Hawks had to wear suits according to Aldo. Aldo also insisted that Vito carry a gun again since lately they were having trouble with the Latin Kings from Jersey City. Vito was

---

19 Siggies--- slang for Sicilians

nervous about this because of all the trouble they recently had with the police. But Aldo was serious and was getting more and more demanding as president of the club. He was becoming more threatening in his manner since he knew that he had Joey Messina behind him. With the Messina's behind the Hawks, they had to pay tribute. Don Franco Messina had said, "If you want to be a gangster in my town, you have to pay me for the privilege." So now, the Black Hawks had to start up more enterprises to raise money for the privilege of operating in Hoboken, New Jersey.

Other than this new turn of events things were working out fine. Detectives Gilligan, Metcalfe and the other cops were still hanging around, but he had steeled himself to their presence. Only once had he been disrespectful when he ran into them, and they had taken him down to the station for questioning. For two hours they had interrogated him without being able to shake him from his original story. In frustration, they finally had to release him. Now, he understood that is wasn't profitable to be disrespectful to cops. The only thing he regretted was having visited Father Joe that night, but the priest had kept quiet. When he saw Father Joe at the center, he never again referred to the visit or their conversation.

In reality, Father Joe was waiting for Vito to reopen the subject. But Vito felt sufficiently safe to bury the episode forever. The picture of Joey Pazzo lying on the floor with blood oozing out of his head was less distinct. And to Vito, the shooting became an incident that was just unfortunate, like getting a flat tire or stubbing your toe. Besides, Joey deserved it! He showed his little brother his dick, the frigging pervert! And, he technically did not kill Joey, his brother Dominic did, to save his life, because Joey was choking him to death. Yeah, this was all water under the bridge. Geez, guys were being killed in VietNam every day and no one was making a big deal about them, except for some stupid hippies who no one paid

126

attention to anyway. And, if a guy believed in God, then it was fate that Joey died, although Vito would have preferred that someone else had been chosen to make a stiff of him.

His mother was just setting the table for dinner as he walked into the apartment. "You're on time," she said. "A miracle!"

"I just came from Saint Ann's Center," he lied.

"Go wash up and sit down to eat," His mother said, indifferently. "I want to get done early, because I'm working tomorrow."

"Oh, Momma!" Dominic complained, running out of the bedroom. "Again?! You're working again?!"

His mother hugged him, "I'm sorry, *figlio mio,* but they want me to come in."

Dominic clung to his mother's skirt, "You said you were gonna take me somewhere tomorrow!" There was a treble in his voice. I was gonna wear my new suit. I haven't worn it since Easter Sunday. Vito wears a suit everyday now, like a real gangster!"

Mrs. Fierro glowered at Vito, "Like a real gangster! Do you hear your little brother?! Like a real gangster?! Is this what I work myself to death for, so my son's can be like real gangsters?! This he gets from you, his older brother!"

"From me?!" Vito said, touching his chest. "From me, your gonna blame me for what he says?!"

"Your ideas!!" she yelled at him. " I want to go to work tomorrow, like I want a heart attack!"

"Oh no, here we go again with the yelling and screaming! Will you shut up, fer Christ sake, I can't stand it anymore!"

"You can't stand it?! You can't stand it?! It's me who can't stand it anymore! My two boys, my children are mafiosi!" She put her hands over her face and began to cry. "Is this why we left Sicily, to come to American and my sons become Mafiosi anyway?" She

127

looked up at the Crucifix on the wall overlooking the dining room. "Why, why, why?!" She wailed, beating her chest.

"So, I've got to stay home alone again tomorrow!" Dominic yelled, running into the bedroom cursing. "Son of a bitch, I'm always alone!"

Mrs. Fierro looked at Vito. "Suppose I give you twenty dollars," she began, "would you take your little brother to the movies tonight?"

"I can't, Mom," Vito said.

"And why not?" His mother said, almost snarling at him.

"I have a date tonight, something special."

"Phew," his mother spat at him, "*Vergognoso!*[20] Dates with *Puttane*[21] and *cattive persone*[22]! She waved a wooden spoon she had been stirring the sauce with. "You should be worrying about you brother, your family, not a bunch of *gente de strada*![23]

Vito waved his hand, "You don't know what you're talking about!"

"I don't know what I'm talking about?!" She yelled, "I read the papers! I see that your gang, your friends, were all taken in by the police and charged with criminal activity! I'm not stupid!"

"Yeah, but I didn't get charged with anything!"Vito yelled back.

"A miracle from God!" she barked, waving the wooden spoon at his head. "And you can't take you poor brother to the movies tonight?!"

"I'll take him tomorrow," Vito said. "I swear to God I will!" He spoke to his mother's back, "I would take Dom out tonight, but this is a date I can't get out of. And you shouldn't call her a *puttana*, she's a good girl."

---

20 Vergognoso---Disgraceful.
21 Puttane--- Whores
22 Cattiva Persone --- Bad people.
23 Gente de strada--- Street people.

"Is she Italian?"

"Yes, she is. She's Sicilian like us and a nice girl, I really like her."

His mother shrugged her shoulders, "Sicilian?"

"Yeah, Ma, she's Sicilian, like us."

"Okay, I'll take your brother out after supper if he helps me with the dishes. But tomorrow you gotta do something with him, poor kid, he's always alone."

Dominic lay diagonally across his bed refusing to move when Vito asked him to come for supper. "Fuck you," Dom said to him. "I hate your guts."

"Don't be that way kid," Vito said, distressed. "Mom's gonna take you to the movies tonight and I'm gonna show you a good time tomorrow, okay?"

"You don't have to do shit for me!" Dominic cried.

"No, I want to, really! We always have a good time together, don't we?"

"You don't, you act like I'm a pain in your ass."

"You are!" said Vito, laughing.

"Fuck you, you're an asshole!" spat Dominic.

"Look," Vito reasoned with him, "this isn't getting us anywhere. Come on and eat like a good kid. Mamma's gotta get up early in the morning and go to work." He grabbed Dominic by the hair pulling him off the bed.

Dominic swung around punching Vito in the face. "Don't put your hands on my or I'll ice you like I did Joey!!" He growled.

Vito grabbed him by the throat drawing back his fist. "I'll rap your teeth down your throat if you talk like that again," He whispered tersely. "You gotta keep your mouth shut about that, I told you before!" He shook his brother hard slapping him across the face. "Don't you understand yet?!"

"Yes, yes, yes!" Dominic cried.

"Now, come on. Come eat, and tomorrow well have a good time."

As they ate, Dominic spoke of his loneliness. He was tired of going to Saint Ann's Center and playing basketball and checkers with nerdy church kids; sitting alone watching television at night. At ten years old, the world had it axis around his mother, brother, and father who was in prison. There was no compensation for their voluntary or involuntary neglect. His only escape was walking the neighborhood hanging out with the other latchkey kids who haunted the streets at night. He was now used to the tumult of downtown Hoboken with it shouts, cries and curses. The routine of walking from the center to the tenement house in which he lived, seeing Gypsy women holding their infant girls over the curb as they urinated, watching boys his age chase one another around the neighborhood screaming obscenities; the storefront clubs that the street gangs and Mafia crews operated out of. He was oblivious to the dirt and refuse that lie in the streets which everyone took for granted. Each and everyday, as he walked the streets, he became harder and harder to the rottenness and violence that permeated his neighborhood.

Vito wiped the dishes rapidly as his brother handed them to him, stacking them on the washboard. He had plenty of time before he had to meet Angela at ten o'clock. If he could have had his way, he wouldn't go to the dance at all. But he had sold his quota of tickets and he knew that the Black Hawks expected every member to be present. Ever since the guys had been arrested and Aldo had gotten in with Joey Messina, things had changed, especially with Aldo. Now, he bossed the guys around not permitting himself to be questioned in any decision he made, for he was obsessed with the idea of clearing each member and becoming a made man with the Messina family. Thus, Aldo Pinto demanded complete obedience from each Black Hawk. Vito was often tempted to tell Aldo that he was dropping out of the gang, but he knew if he did he would never be safe on the street. He would be a guy without backup and a guy without backup was a dead man, a victim to any gang who wanted to mess with him.

Aldo never threatened to kill anyone, but everyone knew that to become an actual made man you had to make your bones or have a killing under your belt. No matter how often he was reassured, the sight of Detectives Gilligan or Metcalfe questioning members of the gang would send Aldo into a tailspin of violent rage. After the detectives would leave, Aldo would accuse Vito of being too flippant, or talking too much or too little. Aldo never actually threatened to kill Vito, but the manner in which he looked at him made Vito's back turn to ice. To make matters worse, not for a moment did Vito doubt that Mikey Sabatelli hated him and wanted to turn him in, in the worst way. For he considered Vito and his brother the reason for his and the gang's crushing legal problems.

As he concentrated on washing the dishes and trying not to worry, his mother came in from cleaning off the dining room table.

"Oh jeez, here she comes," Vito moaned, "now it starts again."

"Remember, I'm your mother and I can give you a good slap in the face," she said.

Vito moved out of his mother's range, "I was only kidding, Ma."

"Your kidding has got you into a lot of trouble already."

"*Porco miseria!*" Vito threw down the sponge, "You're never gonna forget this shit, are you?"

"Its not easy to forget!" His mother yelled. "Everyday, I'm reminded of it! People where I work are constantly asking me about it!" She shook her head, musing, "Funny, if you were getting good grades in school nobody would even bother asking me. But because they think my son is a gangster, I've got plenty of people interested in my business."

"Ma, I'm not a gangster!"

"You tell me a big lie! I know gangsters! I grew up in Sicily, I can smell a Mafiosio! Those Black Birds or Hawks or whatever you call them are Mafiosio! Believe me, I know!"

"They're all okay guys," said Vito, angrily. "They just got a tough break, that's all."

"I don't know what's gonna become of you," Mrs. Fierro said, rubbing a steel wool pad against the inside of a cast iron pot. "I don't understand you. Not for years, have I had a clue what you are doing. Ever since your father made you wear that cheap confirmation suit. Somehow," she faced her son while rinsing out the pot under hot water, "You've never forgiven us for that. Remember, *figlio mio*, no matter how much you suffered, it's worse for me. You'll understand if you ever have children."

Vito was ashamed to look at his mother. She was such a good woman. She worked so hard to keep a roof over their heads. With his father in jail, it was harder for her than Vito could have imagined. She worked double shifts, never got any sleep and worried about her two sons always being left alone. "Don't worry Ma, I'll change, you'll see."

"I'll finish," she said. "Go get dressed for your date. Where are you going?"

"To a small party," Vito said, "nothing special."

132

Chapter 17

As Vito and Angela stepped out of a cab in front of the Union Club, Vito noticed four large young men whom he had never seen before. Without speaking, they examined his tickets and nodded for them to enter. In their presence, one felt the threat of impending violence. Vito knew immediately that they were members of the Messina family who were sent to act as security for the dance. No one entering the dance would be fool hearty enough to challenge their authority.

Aldo Pinto stood at the checkroom counter behind which Blackie was handling the coat check.

"You're late," Aldo said to Vito after curtly acknowledging his introduction to Angela.

Vito took Angela's hand and led her into the club room. "So what, the dance is gonna be a flop because I'm late?!" He called over his shoulder to Aldo.

Aldo looked at Blackie and shook his head. "He's getting to be a friggin wise guy, isn't he?"

"I know," said Blackie. "I don't know what he's trying to prove."

"Trying to be a big man in front of his girlfriend," Aldo said, frowning, "and believe me, I'm not forgetting it."

Vito and Angela wove their way through the crowd on the dance floor towards the bandstand as Vito looked around for someone he knew. He waved to Tony Corizzi, who was leaning against the wall smoking a cigarette.

"I want you to meet my girl," he said to Tony. "Angela, this is Tony, he's a Hawk."

Tony dropped his cigarette crushing it underfoot. "Hello," he said, looking Angela up and down admiringly. "Glad to know ya!"

"Where are the rest of the guys," Vito asked.

" They're circulating around. I'm waiting for my date. She's in the ladies room."

"How's the dance going?" Vito asked, looking over at Blackie who was mad as hell because he didn't have a date, because Anna had dropped him since the police had questioned her.

"Pretty good," Tony replied. "The crowd sure is coming in, but they're leaving too which is good so it don't get too crowded, ya know? See that guy over there?" He pointed to a slim, tough-looking guy about twenty years old with a face as thin and deadly as the blade of an axe. "That's Frankie Messina. He'll go into action if there's any trouble."

"Who is he?" asked Angela, taken aback by his demeanor.

"Like I said, that's Frankie Messina. A real hard guy from the Messina clan. I saw him go into action about an hour ago," Tony went on. "He sure cleaned up a guy who was trying to crash the dance without a ticket. Man, did he do a fast job on him. I tell ya, he's is a tough son of a bitch, man!" Tony called to him, "Frankie, come here for a minute will ya?!"

Frankie Messina detached himself from the wall and walking slowly towards them. "What's the trouble?" He asked Tony in a low pitched voice that sounded like sharp slivers of ice.

"No trouble." Tony explained. "I want you to meet another one of our gang. Frank Messina, this is Vito Fierro, one of our guys. And this is his girl, Angela, isn't it?" He said turning to her.

"That's right," Angela said, "Hello."

"Vito and his date can stay all night," Tony told Frankie.

"I'll remember," Frankie said, "You wanna dance?" He asked Angela.

Angela started to speak but stopped.

"Sure,"Tony nudged Vito, "go ahead Angela, dance with him."

"You don't mind?" Frankie asked Vito.

"No," Vito replied. "Go ahead."

Vito watched as Frankie led Angela onto the dance floor in a slow dance, pulling her close to him.

"What's the big idea?" Vito said, looking at Tony.

"The Messina family is helping us out, we gotta show them a good time."

Vito curled his upper lip. "So, you show them a good time with your girl!"

"I am!" Tony replied calmly, "Frankie's friend is in the backroom right now with my date."

Vito grabbed Tony by the lapels of this jacket, pulling him close. "Listen buddy," he said. "Angela isn't that kind of a date. She's my girlfriend! I'm not letting nobody put their hands on her for you, the club, or anybody else! I don't give a flying fuck if he's a Messina or not! Get it!"

"Take your hands off me you bastard!" Tony whispered angrily. "Do you wanna start a riot? This dance has got to go smoothly."

Vito released him and stepped back.

Tony smoothed the lapels of his jacket and looked Vito in the eyes as he spoke. "I'm not forgetting this, V. I'll take care of you some other time."

"Fuck you!" Vito snarled, spinning around as he felt someone's hand on his sleeve. It was Blackie.

"Where's Angela?" he asked.

Vito's hand trembled as he lit a cigarette. "She's dancing with some hard guy from the Messina tribe."

"It looks like the dance is going over big." Blackie waved, as Aldo walked by giving Vito a critical look.

The music stopped as the band stopped for a break. Vito rushed into the crowd to find Angela. She was standing in the center of the floor, laughing at something Frankie Messina had said to her.

"I was bringing your date back to you." Frankie's voice was so low that Vito had to strain to hear him.

"Thanks! "Come on," Vito said, taking Angela's arm, "let's get outta here, this dance sucks!"

"But I like it," Angela protested. "We just got here! You told me so much about he Black Hawks and now you want to go?!"

"Well, it's too damn hot in here and the cigarette smoke is killing me," Vito insisted.

"So, let's go sit in the anteroom where it's cooler. Come on, please?" Angela coaxed him.

"All right," Vito said sullenly. "We'll stay, but I wanna go in an hour or so."

The band started up once more playing "Summer in the City" by The Loving Spoonful. "I like this song," said Angela smiling.

"I hate it!" complained Vito, " A bunch of long haired hippies! Let them come to Hoboken and they'll get their hippy asses kicked!"

"So negative tonight," Angela replied, looking sad.

"Aw, I'm sorry. I just didn't like that Frankie guy slow dancing with you."

"Oh, don't be jealous, it was just a dance." Angela leaned over kissing Vito's cheek. She stood up and with her arms outstretched invited Vito to dance. Vito had to smile, she looked so pretty standing there moving her hips to the music. He took her out onto the dance floor as the beat became louder. The hit song "Good Loving" blared as the dancing became more unruly and violent. Vito and Angela saw two more of his gang on the dance floor quietly tapping couples and suggesting that they leave. Most of the couples left immediately, but one boy refused becoming belligerent. As he pulled back his fist to slug one of the Black Hawks, Frankie Messina stepped forward hitting the boy with a short uppercut to the jaw. His head snapped back and he hit the floor with a thud. The girl opened her mouth to scream but Frankie stepped behind her placing his hand over her mouth. The boy got up off the floor and moved toward Frankie but stopped short as he saw the open knife in Frankie Messina's right hand. Without any further fight, the couple allowed themselves to be escorted out of the Union Club.

"That Frankie is a real hard guy!" Angela said.

"What, you like him?" Vito snapped at her.

"I didn't say I did," she retorted. "Gee, you're touchy tonight."

"Aw, shut up!" Vito turned away from her. "Go with him if you want to!"

Angela's eyes filled with tears. "What's the matter? I didn't do anything."

"Forget it!" Vito led her off the dance floor. "I'm sorry, I just didn't like you dancing with him. He was holding you pretty close and you were smiling and it looked like you were digging it."

"But I don't like him, I was just trying to be nice." Angela insisted. "Let's stop it," she said. "We don't want to have our first fight, do we?"

At that moment, Blackie approached them, staggering slightly, asking Angela to dance with him. "Go ahead!" Vito replied, turning his back on them in disgust. He sat on the arm of one of the easy chairs and reflected that the dance was not as he had expected it to be.

Blackie returned with Angela, and Vito knew immediately by her loose laugh that she had taken a stiff drink with Blackie. She giggled as Blackie patted her on the ass while pushing her towards Vito. Blackie took out a silver flask of whiskey. "Want some?" he asked Vito.

Vito's eyes became narrow slits. "What are you doing touching my girl's ass?"

"Oh, it's nothing!" Angela laughed.

"Shut up!" Vito snarled at her. "Give me that bottle!" he said to Blackie, holding out his hand.

"You want a drink?"

"No, I'm gonna empty it in the can!"

Blackie put the flask back in his pocket. "Like hell you are!"

"Come over here," Vito said, pulling Blackie into a corner of the room. "I'm warning you to ditch that bottle! You're drunk and I don't like the way you're acting!"

"What the fuck do you care how I'm acting. I can hold my liquor!"

Vito held out his hand, "Now give me that bottle."

"Suppose I don't want to?" Blackie clutched his hip pocket.

"Shut up and give me that bottle or else!"

"Don't tell me to shut up." Blackie staggered a little, "I don't trust you! The other guys don't either, they all think you're a fucking rat!"

Vito slapped Blackie across the face pushing him down into a chair. Angela rushed over and grabbing Vito's arm. He pushed her away telling her to sit down and mind her own business. Looking at Blackie, he said, "Listen, I know that you're drunk. If you don't give me that bottle, I'm gonna call Aldo and Tony and we're all gonna knock the shit outta ya!"

Aldo came over with Frankie Messina and Tony.

"Blackie's drunk!" Vito explained to them. "He's grabbing my girl's ass right in front of me!"

"Oh, it's no big deal!" cried Angela.

Vito turned to her yelling, "Shut the fuck up, I said!"

Angela started to cry. Frankie Messina took Angela by the arm sitting her down and giving her his handkerchief to wipe her eyes. He turned to Vito saying quietly, "So, let him get drunk. He's having a good time. As long as he's not bothering anybody."

Vito released Blackie and turned around. He approached Frankie Messina, staring directly into his eyes which did not blink. "Listen," he began, "the guys've been telling me that you're a hard guy. Wait!" he raised his hand to prevent Frankie from interrupting him, "maybe you are, you're a Messina, okay, good! But, I'm a hard guy too. I don't like you, and if you make a move for that shiv of yours, I'm gonna beat the piss outta you!"

Aldo stepped between Vito and Frankie. "Cut it out guys," he pleaded. "We don't want no trouble."

Vito struggled to keep his head. He knew that Frankie had what he lacked: the ability to present the outward appearance of calm at all times. No matter how Frankie Messina felt, whether he seethed with anger and rage, with the lust to stab or kill, his expressionless eyes and tightly compressed lips never betrayed him. While threatening a guy or beating him, Frankie's countenance never changed. Now, as he listened to Vito's threat he kept his hand in the deep pocket of his double-breasted jacket, tense and alert for a sudden attack, as always master of himself. He was a true Messina. The deadly quiet ingrained in him from his earliest youth emanated from his very presence.

"I'm not starting any trouble," Vito went on. "But I want him to stay away from my date. I saw him over there talking to her, and now he's over here telling me what to do with Blackie. Now You!" He turned to Blackie again, "Give me that bottle and be quick about it before you have an accident!"

"Give him the bottle!" Aldo ordered.

Blackie withdrew the bottle from his pocket. "I'm just giving it to you because Aldo says so, not because you told me to!" He glared at Vito. "But I'm not forgetting this disrespect, understand!?"

Suddenly, they heard Mikey Sabatelli's voice pitched in a key that meant he was seeking trouble. "Don't give it to him, Blackie," he said. "Give it to me and let's see if he can take it away from me!"

"Shut up!!" Aldo turned to him, "get the hell outta here, I just got everything calmed down!"

Mikey turned and walked away at Aldo's command, but turned glaring at Vito. "You got yours coming brother, believe me, it's coming!"

"Yeah, go fuck yourself, you piece of shit!" Vito responded. "I kicked your ass once, ya wanna try again scumbag!"

Aldo grabbed Vito. "Stop! I mean it, knock it off!"

Vito calmed down and walked over to Angela. In the meantime, with a show of great cordiality Aldo took Frankie Messina's arm leading him to the cloakroom. He spoke earnestly to him, laughing, placing his arm around his shoulder in an effort to convince him that the previous unpleasant scenario meant nothing.

"What's the matter?" Angela asked Vito as he rejoined her.

"Nothing, I just saw you talking to that Messina jerk. Stay away from him if you want to be with me, that's all!"

"He came over and talked to me," Angela said. "He didn't say anything off color or get fresh."

"I know that kind of guy," Vito told her. "He doesn't say anything, and the next thing you know you're flat on your back wondering how you got there."

"Oh, you're making such a big deal out of nothing. You want to go?" She asked him.

"And what about Blackie putting his hand on your ass?"

Angela threw her eyes in the air. "He's drunk and I didn't even feel him do it. Can you just forget about it now and let's go!"

Vito looked around, "Okay, let's blow this joint. I'm sick of it."

It was after twelve o'clock and the mob of new ticket holders were arriving. The Hawks who came stag stood at the door with the Messina boys checking tickets. As Vito escorted Angela out of the door of the Union Club, Mikey pushed forward jostling him.

"Stay away from me," Vito warned him.

Mikey who was obviously drunk, bobbed up and down working himself into a rage. "Who the hell asked you to come to our dance?" Mikey said to him.

Vito did not reply.

"Does your mommy know you're down here? Or how about your father? Does he get laid in prison by a big nigger?" Mikey went on and on as the other Hawks stood by listening. "Yeah," Mikey yelled, "his old man is in the joint getting humped by niggers!"

Vito shoved Mikey into two of the Hawks, "You keep my old man out of this, you stupid bastard!!"

"Does your mother still suck dick to bring money home while your father's in the joint? Ha, ha, ha, ha, is your mama turning tricks on the corner?"

"I'm remembering this," Vito said, trying to imitate Frankie's impassivity.

"I'm not forgetting what I already know about you and your brother. Remember that, you motherfucker!" Mikey continued.

Vito squared off seeing the challenging look in Mikey's eyes. "Come on, you fucking sissy, come on if ya want another beating," Vito dared him.

Aldo came out the door towards them. "Cut it out!" he yelled.

"I'm not doing nothing!" Mikey yelled. "Look at him, he's starting trouble!"

"You're a rat bastard, you were born a rat bastard, you're living like a rat bastard and you're gonna die a rat bastard!" Vito screamed back at him.

Mikey spit at him, "Beat it! You're not a Black Hawk anymore!"

"Go to hell!" Vito said.

"You're not one of us!" Mikey went on, obviously seething with rage. "You don't hang around with us anymore! You got all of us in trouble and we don't want you around! Do we guys?!" He asked the Hawks who stood around them.

The guys were silent and Vito could feel their hostility towards him.

"He don't get it!" Mikey said, looking at Vito with disgust and hate.

"No, I get it!" Vito said, "I guess after tonight, I'm not one of you guys anymore! Now I know where I stand! You'd take this asshole's side over me!" He said looking at the other Black Hawks.

"Who you calling an asshole?!" Mikey said, rushing Vito in a black rage. Vito threw a murderous right cross that hit Mikey in the side of the head. As hard as Vito hit him, that's how hard Mikey's head hit the pavement. Angela screamed as blood spit out of Mikey's nose and ears.

The other Black Hawks grabbed Vito from behind holding him back from kicking Mikey while he was down. Vito struggled to get free, still wanting to inflict punishment on his antagonist.

"What the hell is happening here?! I'm breaking my ass in there and you guys are out here making trouble! Now, what the hell happened to Mikey?! Did you hit him again?!" Aldo yelled, looking at Vito.

"He came at me!" Vito said, "I was defending myself!"

"Get inside!" Aldo pushed him, "We'll take care of Mikey. Geez, you guys are more trouble than you're worth, I swear to God you are!"

Vito pushed passed Aldo still trying to get at Mikey. "I'm gonna kill the fuck!" He said, still in a fury.

Aldo grabbed Vito's arm squeezing it. "Listen to me," he cautioned him. "What's between you and Mikey can be settled some other time. I need you inside to work the floor."

Aldo, Vito and Angela returned to the dance. Angela was noticeably shaken over the violence. "What happened to that kid you hit?" she asked. "He was bleeding out of his nose and ears. I think you really hurt him."

"Forget it!" ordered Vito angrily, "the other guys will take care of him!"

"Don't snap at me!" said Angela, visibly upset, "I was just worried about what happened to him."

"Like I said, forget it!"

"You know what?" Angela said, "I'm going home right now, and don't bother to escort me! You're rude and abusive! I'm tired of trying to be nice to you!" She turned and walked out onto Hudson Street, hailing a passing cab.

Vito ran after her blocking her entrance into the taxi. "Please, Angela, I'm sorry! But you see what just happened, I was still angry over Mikey."

"I don't care! You talk like that to me in front of everyone?! If you want a tramp go inside there's plenty of them in there!" She said, pointing to the Union Club door. "Now, let me pass!" She opened the door of the cab and got in.

Vito watched as the cab drove away. As he turned around Mikey was facing him, gritting his teeth in anger. "You bastard! You suckered me!"

"Listen Mikey," Vito didn't feel like any more drama, since he was crestfallen over Angela leaving. "Why don't you get the hell outta here before I really kick the shit outta you?"

With a smooth rapid motion, Mikey pulled out his switchblade knife, simultaneously pressing the spring and shoving the blade against Vito's stomach. "One move outtta you and this'll be in your guts!" Mikey rasped. "Just one move!"

"Don't move Vito!" One of the Black Hawks warned him. "I'm going to get Aldo!"

Mikey pressed the point of his knife into Vito making a little impression in the cloth of Vito's jacket. "In your guts!" Mikey repeated. "You son of a bitch, you think I can't handle five guys like you?"

"Put that knife down and I'll take you apart!" Vito gasped, trying to move away from the knife, but Mikey pressed the point of the blade deeper into Vito's stomach.

"Nobody suckers me and gets away with it!" Mikey told him, and Vito began to look sick. Mikey's reputation of being a stabber and potential killer was well known on the street. In one of his murderous rages, Mikey was a berserk street and gang fighter, who was spoken of with respect. Impervious to pain and blows, he would keep charging in the middle of any brawl, kicking and slugging with a furry and energy that was unusual. Many on the street predicted that Mikey would be a big time mobster if he lived long enough.

Perspiration dampened Vito's face and his eyes became scared and sick, for the knife pierced his jacket and shirt. He could feel the blade puncturing the skin of his stomach. He realized that any sudden movement might make Mikey drive the knife into his stomach.

"Let's talk this over," said Vito to Mikey.

"Talk over this!" Mikey said, putting his hand on Vito's shoulder while pushing the knife deeper. "You suckered me! Now, you wanna talk?! Well, talk to this you fucking prick!" Vito could feel the blade piercing his stomach.

The crowd opened as Aldo shoved his way towards Mikey and Vito.

"Mikey" – Aldo spoke quietly – "what do you think you're doing?"

"I'm gonna cut this bastard wide open!" Mikey continued to stare at Vito. The blood thirsty look on Mikey's face made the crowd go silent. Any sudden noise, sound, or movement meant that Mikey would sink the blade into Vito's stomach.

Vito's eyes were frantic with fear. His mouth twitched and he kept his arms rigidly at his sides.

"Put the knife down!" Aldo commanded Mikey.

Mikey gritted his teeth, "I'm gonna put it in this rat bastard's belly!"

Aldo put his hand lightly on Mikey's arm. "I need you inside, to help me with the dance," he whispered in Mikey's ear. "I have a girl in the backroom who want's you. She told me she thinks you're hot.

Now, if you stab him, the cops will come and take you away. You won't get laid tonight. You wont get laid for a long time. Now, put the knife down and come inside with me. I'll take care of Vito for suckering you. Okay, now put the blade down, okay?"

Slowly almost imperceptibly, Mikey withdrew the knife. He looked questioningly at Aldo, and Aldo nodded affirmatively.

"Now, put it away," said Aldo, as Mikey closed the knife and put it in his pocket. "Go in the back room, the girl is waiting for you." Mikey gave Vito one last look as he disappeared into the Union Club.

Vito's face was pallid and streaked with perspiration as he straightened his tie trying to look casual.

"I can't figure you out," Aldo said, looking Vito up and down. "You used to be a good guy. Now, you go around fighting with the guys in the gang. I know what's worrying you, but I told you that I ain't gonna spill. I promised you that I would make sure that Mikey would keep his mouth shut. But when you sucker a guy in front of everybody, what do you expect a guy to do?"

Vito turned from him, walking away.

Aldo grabbed his arm spinning him around. "You must think you're a hard guy," he pushed Vito in the chest, "But you're taking on an awful load, trying to be hard with me!" Aldo said menacingly, "I let a lot pass with you already!"

"I'm getting out of here!" Vito said, turning to leave.

"No you're not, you're staying here, I got work for you to do!"

"I wanna go see where my girl is, she just walked out on me because of that idiot Mikey!"

"I said, you're staying here! You gotta help, I hardly been outta of that coat check all night!"

"I'm leaving!" yelled Vito, "try and stop me!"

"Listen wise guy!" Aldo shoved Vito against the building. "You watch what you're saying or I'll fuck you up! You've been running your mouth all night, and I'm one guy that knows that I can kick the crap outta you! Now you're staying! If you wanna look for your girl after the dance is over, that's up to you! But as for now you're staying!"

Vito remembered Frankie Messina and the way he controlled himself. So, instead of yelling back at Aldo, he silently determined that after tonight he was through with the Black Hawks. Two weeks ago, he had been happy that the Hawks were willing to reinstate him as a member in good standing. But now, he was adamant in his resolve to break with them. After what happened tonight, he was sure that he could drop them without regret.

When he spoke his voice was controlled and nonchalant. "All right, Aldo. I'll stay and help out."

Frankie Messina and his boys were losing control over the crowd. The Black Hawks had sold tickets to clubs and gangs that prided themselves on not backing down from anyone. Against one wall of the room, the Marion Boys from Jersey City had isolated two of the Black Hawks and were slapping them around. Frankie struggled to break through the ring of Marion Boys but stopped when one of the Marion Boys, a big six footer with a broken nose and a scar that extended from his temple to his chin, brandished an iron rod in his hand inviting Frankie to step forward and have his head split open.

"You want me to plug him?" One of the Messina boys asked Frankie, pulling a pistol from his jacket pocket.

Frankie shook his head. "The cops'll be here if you do." He looked at the Marion boy. "Why don't you cut it out? We don't want no trouble here."

"We're not shelling out twenty dollars to hang out here for an hour, and then you telling us we gotta leave!" The Jersey City boy said, "We don't take that crap from no one, least of all from a fuck like you!"

"You don't know who you're fucking with!" Frankie said.

"Why, who'd you ever kill?" The Marion boy swung the iron rod threateningly. "I never seen your picture in the post office."

Aldo walked over to the Marion boy, "Hey Angelo, why don't you guys break it up. You're spoiling the dance."

"When we get good and ready! We're from Jersey City! We don't take any crap from Hoboken trash!" Angelo and his Marion boys pushed Frankie Messina and his guys into the center of the dance floor, as their right hands went into their pockets.

Frankie Messina shook his head calmly. He looked at the big Jersey City boy and said, "Angelo, is that your name? You tell your guys to back off or they'll all be found in the East Rutherford Meadows tomorrow morning. You're not dealing with just me. You're dealing with the Messina family, understand?"

The Marion boy laughed, "Who the hell is afraid of the Messina family? Get the hell outta here before my boys beat your brains out!"

Frankie Messina said nothing as he placed a restraining hand on one of the Messina boys. He looked steadily at this Angelo from Jersey City, memorizing each of his features. For this Angelo was now marked to die, and soon. A day, two days, a week, a month, but soon Angelo from Jersey city would be buried in the East Rutherford Meadows. The eyes in Frankie Messina's head shone like bright sparks as he smiled; for he would still be alive when Angelo's head would be blown off of his shoulders. There was no alternative. No lesser punishment would appease Frankie Messina. He had to prove to other would-be hard guys that shoving a Messina around was a swift way to invite death. As Angelo from the Marion Section of

148

Jersey City stood there brandishing the iron rod, cursing and full of fight, he did not realize that soon his parents would be forever wondering what happened to their son. The East Rutherford Meadowlands was a vast swamp of reeds and mud that extended ten thousand acres serving as a graveyard for bodies killed by mobsters from all over North Jersey.

Chapter 18

Joey Messina entered the dance with his gorgeous date as a hush fell over the crowd. It was as if royalty deigned to mingle with the peasants. He walked over to shake hands with Aldo, showing everyone present that Aldo was "numero uno" in the street pecking order.

"Thanks for showing up," said Aldo, almost genuflecting.

"Well, I got some of my cousins here," replied Joey, nodding his head towards Frankie and the others. "I gotta make sure that they're doing a good job."

"They're doing a great job," replied Aldo, smiling. "That Frankie is the real deal. The Black Hawks can't thank you and your family enough for helping us out."

"Just keep up the good work on the street," said Joey, "show that you're a good earner and before you know it, you'll be a Messina. Then nobody can touch you, not even the Pope!"

"I really look forward to that day," Aldo gushed, looking admiringly at Joey.

Joey took his date by the hand leading her to the dance floor. "Man, this place is crowded," he complained, looking at Aldo.

Immediately, Aldo called out to Vito, "Hey, get the guys to clear the floor! Mr. Messina wants to dance!" Each word that Aldo uttered was like the stroke of a bell, booming, decisive and final. Like the parting of the Red Sea, the dance floor was cleared. Vito ran his hand through his hair, there was no quitting the Black Hawks now; at least not until he could disappear completely, but he needed money for that. He shook his head as he watched Joey Messina dancing on the large dance floor with his date, as the other guests stood watching silently. Was there another world other than this? Vito didn't know and honestly did not know how to find out. Two years ago his dream was to become a Black Hawk, the main feeder club into the Messina family, but now just being in their presence made him feel sick. A primordial compulsion to flee welled up in him like a tidal wave but there was no where to run. He leaned against the wall his face the color of white paste.

"What's up with you?" asked Aldo, walking up to him.

Vito opened his mouth gulping. "You guys don't want me here any more, I can tell. Everybody thinks I'm a rat. But you know the real deal, you know the truth."

Aldo put his hand on Vito's shoulder, shaking his head. "You don't have to worry about us. You're a Hawk and we're Hawks. You play square with the boys and you got nothing to worry about, understand? No one quits the Black Hawks, remember, blood in, blood out?"

Vito nodded at Aldo.

Aldo looked Vito in the eyes. "Say it, blood in, blood out!"

"Blood in, blood out!" Vito repeated.

Aldo winked, "Good, now you got it brother!" He turned and walked away.

As the bus rumbled to another rocky stop, Vito's stomach turned as if he were going to puke. He was heading towards the Village in Manhattan to pick up a pound of weed for the Hawks to sell on the street. He hated these damn city buses but Aldo had sent him on this pick-up run into Greenwich Village to meet with some drug dealers and now he was stuck doing these runs every week. He got off at the next stop and decided to walk a couple of blocks to the pick up point.

As he stepped down from the bus on to the sidewalk, he could feel the nausea rising up in his throat. As he reconstructed the dance in his overtired and overtaxed mind, he could see every scene in its true tawdriness. If only he could have taken Angela home and left the dance before the fight started with Mikey, before Aldo had the chance to tie him down to the Black Hawks like a prison sentence. He knew that it was only a matter of time before the cops would question his little brother Dominic. He was worried about what the kid might say. He kept telling himself that he wasn't the one who actually killed Joey and that it was Dominic who pulled the trigger. However, he was an accomplice. He had gone up to Joey's apartment and pushed open the door, that in and of itself was breaking and entry. Not to mention that Joey was shot in the head with his gun. Why the cops hadn't questioned Dominic yet was a mystery to him and constantly worrying about it was making him sick.

Vito walked up to the tenement house where he was supposed to pick up a valise filled with a pound of marijuana. He rang the door bell of the basement floor apartment. The door was answered by a long haired stoned out looking white dude in a tie dyed shirt, ragged blue jeans and worn out sneakers. Rock music was blasting from the apartment as the bleary-eyed hippie let him in. The apartment was an absolute mess with mattresses all over the floor and strobe lights flashing on posters depicting The Rolling Stones and other rock groups. Messy looking hippie girls sat on the floor with equally messy guys smoking weed out of a huge bong. Vito looked completely out of place with his gold jewelry, Italian knit shirt, matching pants and black straw loafers.

"I'm here to pick up the weed for the Black Hawks," he said to the bleary-eyed stoner dude.

"Ah, yeah, cool, we got it here for ya," said the long haired dude, pulling out a valise and handing it to Vito. "Ya got the dough, man?"

Vito produced an envelop from his pocket and handed it to the hippie. "Count it, it's all there," he said.

"No need brother," the villager slurred, "wanna puff a little before ya go?"

Vito looked around at the messy surroundings. "Na, that's alright, thanks anyway, but I gotta get back to Jersey." He picked up the valise, turned and left as the song "She's a Rainbow" blasted behind him. Considering his neighborhood and experience, his preferences were Frank Sinatra, Tony Bennett, Frankie Valli and the Four Seasons. He was completely out of his element with this noisy, screaming discordant music these hippies listened to. However, he had gotten what he had come for and that was all he cared about at the moment. These hippies or whatever you called them boggled his mind. Why anyone would wear ripped clothing and not even comb their hair. And the girls looked like homeless skanks; no make up, no nylon stockings or pretty sun dresses to make them look desirable. As he sat on the bus back to Jersey, he laughed to himself thinking of these strange individuals that hung out in Greenwich Village.

Chapter 19

Detective Lieutenant Brian Gilligan spat at the headline of The Jersey Journal, tore the offending paper in two, and threw the halves into the wastebasket. He just couldn't seem to get a break in this damn Joey Pazzo murder case. He looked at his detectives Metcalfe, Fiori and Sweeney, whose faces were flat pictures of gloom.

"We never get a break," Metcalfe said. "Not one single break. How the hell did this get in the paper?" He pointed to the wastebasket.

Sweeney shrugged his shoulders, "How do I know? We kept it quiet. After all, it was only a hunch."

"But a good hunch," Fiori agreed. "You suggested that we try dragging the river near the piers because maybe the killer got rid of the gun there."

Gilligan nodded sadly, "So I was right!"

"Yep," Fiori continued. "The second try with the dredge on the 11th Street Pier and up comes this pistol with the same rifling as the bullet that killed Joey Pazzo."[24]

"So, I still don't know how the freaking newspapers got wind of it," Gilligan fumed. "These kids are slick. There aren't any fingerprints on the revolver. But I'd bet my right nut that we got the right kid who did it. Now, he'll see it in the paper and when we pick the little bastard up, he'll have another good alibi. Damn it!! It really burns me up. I know that that Vito Fiero kid is in on this shit some how."

"It would have been sweet to spring the gun on him and see his reaction," Metcalfe said.

"Well," Gilligan sighed, "We'd better send out a call to pick him up anyway."

"Pick up his little brother too," said Metcalfe. "The kid sure looked upset the day of the murder."

Vito shivered as he sat in Turks Palace Candy Store reading and rereading the headline in the "Jersey Journal" newspaper. They had found the gun. Now, the police had the weapon. How certain could he be that there weren't his or his brother's fingerprints on it? He could no longer be certain of anything, for who would have dreamed

---

24   **Rifling marks** are spiral grooves which improve the aerodynamic stability of the **bullet** and they are shaped or cut into the barrel of the gun allowing the police to match the gun with the bullet.

that the cops would find the gun after so many weeks? Now, the cops had the gun. They had fished it out of the Hudson River near the 11ᵗʰ Street Pier. How much other shit must there be in that freaking river and they pulled up his pistol?! What were the chances?!

Vito sat erect on the counter stool of the candy store staring into his soda glass. This meant that the cops had doubted the Black Hawk's stories and had decided to drag the channels. Now, they had proof! Vito felt himself going limp, his heart began to pound violently, beating and thumping with fright. They were caught; trapped! Dominic, his own brother, had put him on this hook; had made him an accomplice in this murder! It wouldn't be long now before the cops would pick them up again, sweating them until they confessed. Aldo and Mikey know the truth because of Dominic, that stupid little jerk, who thinks he's some kind of mob guy now because he pulled the trigger. If the cops pick anybody up again, someone will spill and he'll be done and go to jail like his father; and his little brother Dominic will go to reform school. His poor mother will die of a broken heart. His saintly mother, who works like a slave to keep her family together. He couldn't stand it, the thought of what would happen to her being all alone with no one. Vito sprung off the counter stool. The cops were too close.

"Let's see your paper," Willy Quack called to him. "I hear they found the rod that knocked off Joey Pazzo."

Vito handed him the paper, "Keep it," he said.

"Hey," Willy called to him, "I'll give it right back, where ya going?"

Vito closed the door of the candy store behind him, without replying. What was he going to do? For certain, the cops would be questioning all the Black Hawks again. He had to get out of town, alone, without his little brother; who he knew would crack if the

155

cops sweated him. If only he were certain that there weren't any fingerprints on the gun. But cold reasoning told him that even the lack of fingerprints was not a defense. He was a suspect and he knew that the police would question and sweat every member of the Hawks until Mikey or Aldo or even his brother would crack and then he would be arrested and imprisoned.

Vito moaned in anguish. He was done for and he knew it. He would die in the electric chair, moaning as he was being dragged down the corridor to the death chamber. His little brother would go to a hard-time reformatory. All of his poise, confidence, and reason had left him. He stumbled down Monroe Street, unseeing, his face white and drawn. There wasn't any out for him, nothing. At any moment, he expected to feel a firm hand on his shoulder; a hand that would be the first thing leading to his execution.

As he thought of death, the desire to live became paramount, more dominant, more insistent. Vito began to reason again. Things looked bad for him and his brother. He shut his eyes to eliminate Dominic. Dominic no longer belonged in his thinking. Dominic didn't count any longer because he was a minor; he wouldn't get much of a punishment. So now, only he, Vito Fiero, mattered. He had to figure a way out of this jam, not worry about his little brother, the stupid little prick, opening his big mouth to Aldo and Mikey Sabatelli who hated him. He had to escape and leave all this bullshit behind. But why wait another minute? Why not get out now?

Vito was filled with a renewed sense of hope, as he looked in his wallet; he had thirty dollars. At home, he had about two hundred dollars stashed in the bottom of his dresser drawer. He had to quickly get the money and some clothes. He needed to get the marijuana he had hidden in his room. The weed would calm him, give him clarity of mind, and the courage and focus he needed. As he smoked the reefer, he would think of being tough and not being afraid of anything. The mood would be carried over and exaggerated so that nothing could faze him. He would use some of the money to buy a gun. He was determined to put an end to Mikey, who would surely rat him out. Mikey, that rat bastard, who would do anything to get even with him for beating him up in front of everyone. Then, with the gun, he could stick up a liquor store and get enough money to disappear. He needed the money! He needed a gun! He had to get to New York's Little Italy and buy a gat from the guys he knew there. Then he would get money anyway he could! He'd go to Mexico or Canada, or out west to cattle country where he could get lost and never be found. As long as he left New Jersey, he would be safe. His mind raced uncontrollably as he thought of one plan after another. He would beat this rap! He was too young to die in the chair! And if he had to die, he would go out fighting!

As he ran up the stairs of his tenement house, his irrational hatred for Mikey Sabatelli festered and grew all the stronger. This was Mikey's fault, not his and not his brothers. Mikey, who hated him, would squeal on him. Mikey, who thought he was a hard guy, who thought he could disrespect him. He was the one who would squeal and put him and his brother in prison. Even if he didn't get the chair because he was only an accomplice, there was still prison. Vito saw prison: its gray monotony, its closeness, its stifling confinement, its total lack of freedom. Look how long the month of June had been. How much longer would twenty years be, locked away from living?

He entered his shabby apartment. Dominic was in school and his mother was at work. He was alone and even the thought of Mikey Sabatelli enraged him. Now, he was going to get his comeuppance, the trouble making bastard! He went into his drawer finding the reefer he had stashed away. Since he was alone, he lit up a joint, sat on his bed and sucked in the sweet smoke. As the marijuana took effect, Vito became calmer and a new plan began to formulate in his mind. No, murdering Mikey was not the thing to do. He would turn the tables on this whole case.

"Yes, yes, now Mikey, you are gonna be in the hot seat!" He chuckled to himself. "And Aldo too, both of you are gonna get the fucking chair, not me!" He lept off of his bed running out of the apartment, down the stairs onto the street. "Yeah, yeah, I know exactly what to do!" he muttered to himself as he walked briskly towards "Turk's Candy Store".

He walked into Turk's ignoring Willy at the counter while entering the phone booth. Carefully, he placed his handkerchief across the telephone mouthpiece and dialing the police station number.

"Hello," he said, in a disguised and muffled voice. "I want to speak to Detective Lieutenant Gilligan, it's important." Vito waited as the connection was made. "Hello," he said again, his voice trembling and the telephone receiver damp in his hand. "I want to talk to Lieutenant Gilligan....Yes, Gilligan."

Vito peered out of the booth. The only customers in the store were two boys buying baseball cards. It was vital that no one see him in the phone booth. So, to play it safe he shifted so that he stood with his back against the glass panels of the door. Perspiration dampened his lips and nose as he rubbed them against the handkerchief that covered the mouthpiece. He tensed as he heard Gilligan's voice and gulped before he was able to speak.

"Detective Gilligan," he began, "I'm a witness to Joey Pazzo's murder. I saw the whole thing happen. I wanted to call you before this but I was scared. The guys who knocked off Joey Pazzo are those kids from that Italian street gang, the Black Hawks. They're real killers." Vito mentally congratulated himself. If he played it right, they would arrest Mikey and Aldo. And if they tried to implicate him, he would deny it. That was the angle, the out, Mikey and Aldo were the killers.

At the other end of the telephone, Gilligan signaled for Metcalfe and Fiori to listen in on the extension. He winked at them, the case was breaking. "So, you know who did it?" Gilligan spoke into the phone. "Can you tell us?"

"I can," Vito said, "I saw Aldo Pinto and Mikey Sabatelli go into the Pazzo apartment the day of the murder. Then I heard a gun shot and saw them running out the back into the quadrants. I was afraid to talk before now."

"You don't have to be afraid," Gilligan said, "we'll protect you. Do you want to come down to the station and make a statement?"

"No," Vito faltered. "Their gang is liable to get me. They're killers. I'm telling you who did it and that's all!"

"Okay, so you're saying that Aldo Pinto and Michael Sabatelli killed Joey Pazzo, is that it?"

Vito's mouth was dry and his tongue like sandpaper. He had to go through with this plan. He was now officially a rat, not just a rat, but a rat bastard. He was now someone who squeals on his brothers. "Yes," he said, :it was Aldo Pinto and Mikey Sabatelli!" Vito felt remorseful wanting to retract his words but it was too late.

Detective Gilligan's face was triumphant as he smiled at Detectives Metcalfe and Fiori. "Okay," said Gilligan now playing his trump card. "You'd better come in, Vito. We have your little brother here and he's already told us everything. He's in custody. Your mother is here also. Either you come in voluntarily or I'll send a detachment out to find and arrest you."

Vito slammed the receiver onto the hook, stuffing his handkerchief into his pocket and running out onto the street. He stood on the sidewalk, dazed, turning about, not knowing where to go. There was no escape. Blindly, he ran into the hallway of his tenement and up the stairs. In his stoned haste to implicate Aldo and Mikey, he had forgotten his wallet with the money in it. He flung open the kitchen door with his hands trembling, then he opened the bureau drawer searching under his clothing for his wallet. He sighed with relief and hope as he found it. As he counted out the money, he thought two hundred dollars was so little. He could still afford to buy a gun. He would shoot it out with the cops if he had to. He wasn't going to go to jail for the rest of his life or get the chair. He'd go down fighting, if he had to.

He jerked erect as he heard the apartment door open, turning abruptly he saw his brother Dominic walking into the kitchen.

"Oh," Dominic said, startled, "I didn't know that you were home."

"The cops know that we killed Joey!!" He said to Dominic.

"How?" asked Dominic, "I didn't say nothing to them."

"Did they question you?" asked Vito.

"No, nobody questioned me."

"They didn't pick you up from school?"

"No,."

"You and Mama weren't at the police station?"

"No," said Dominic shaking his head. "What are you talking about?"

The sirens screamed closer as Vito looked around in a frenzy. he stiffened as rage and fear surged through his body. Detective Gilligan had outsmarted him. That son of a bitch Irish bastard had outwitted him. They really never had his brother, but now they knew for sure. He looked out of the apartment window as he heard the sirens peeling down Monroe Street.

"Say goodbye to Mamma for me!" He said, as he opened the window.

"Where are you going?" Dominic called, confused.

"The cops," Vito gasped, "the cops!"

"Don't leave me alone!" cried Dominic, "I'm scared!"

"Scared?! Scared?! You little fool, I'm gonna burn!" Vito's eyes rolled in his head. His tongue flicking his lips, and dumb with fear, he raced out onto the fire escape and onto the flat roof. Cautiously, he peered over the edge seeing squad cars blocking the entrance of the tenement, Crowds of people were coming out of the buildings to see what was going on. Terrified and in anguish, he put his face in his hands thinking of the suspense, fears, and uncertainties that had made his days and nights a nightmare of misery; which had corroded and rotted the guts out of his friendship with the Black Hawks. In his all consuming hatred, he had betrayed and trapped himself beyond all hope of escape. He thought of Angela, of her bright smile, her firm young breasts, her soft lips, whose kiss and caress he would never know again. He thought of freedom, the escape that had eluded him because he falsely accused two innocent brother Hawks. He thought of living in clean fresh air, broad fields and rivers away from the slums of North Jersey, the clean streets and houses he had yearned for and now would never know.

As he stood on the edge of the roof, afraid and uncertain, he suddenly heard the commanding voice of Detective Gilligan, who was pointing a gun at him and telling him to put his hands in the air and lay flat on tarmac roof.

"Leave me alone!" Screamed Vito as he ran to the fire escape. Two uniformed police officers blocked his escape. In a blind rage, Vito rushed the policemen striking blows to their heads and shoulders. The officers grabbed him by the arms and throat as he struggled in a frenzied attempt to escape.

People on the street began to yell and point at the struggling figures on the roof. They could see the thrashing boy desperately fighting the police who fought to contain him. In a desperate explosion of strength and fury, Vito broke free of the arresting officers while attempting to jump the expanse from one roof to the other. As onlookers peered from the surrounding windows, the people screamed while shielding their eyes, afraid to look or see. Yet, they were fascinated at the deadly scenario unfolding on the roof. As Vito desperately leapt across the tenement divide, his foot slipped. Detective Gilligan frantically grasped at Vito, desperately trying to save the boy as he fell, bouncing off of the fire escape and careening through the air smashing onto the pavement.

Stunned, Dominic looked out of the tenement window at his brother's lifeless body lying broken in the trash covered alleyway.

Mrs. Fierro got off of the bus from her shift at work, wondering what the commotion was on Monroe Street.

The End